The Works of
KNUT HAMSUN
Winner of the Nobel Prize for Literature, 1920

NOVELS

HUNGER
(*Sult*) Translated by George Egerton
With an introduction by Edwin Björkman

GROWTH OF THE SOIL
(*Markens Gröde*) Translated, with an essay on Hamsun, by W. W. Worster

PAN
Translated by W. W. Worster
With an introduction by Edwin Björkman

SHALLOW SOIL
(*Ny Jord*) Translated, with an introductory essay, by Carl Christian Hyllested

DREAMERS
(*Svaermere*) Translated by W. W. Worster

WANDERERS
(*Under Höstjaernen* and *En Vendrer Spiller med Sordin*)
Translated by W. W. Worster
With an introduction by Edwin Björkman

VICTORIA
Translated by A. G. Chater

CHILDREN OF THE AGE
(*Börn av Tiden*) Translated by J. S. Scott

SEGELFOSS TOWN (*Segelfoss By*)
Translated by J. S. Scott

A PLAY

IN THE GRIP OF LIFE
Translated by Graham and Tristan Rawson

Benoni

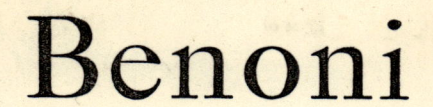

Translated from the Norwegian of
KNUT HAMSUN
by Arthur G. Chater

NEW YORK
Alfred·A·Knopf
MCMXXV

COPYRIGHT, 1925, BY ALFRED A. KNOPF, INC.

MANUFACTURED IN THE UNITED STATES OF AMERICA

Benoni

I

A WOOD stands between the sea and Benoni's house. It is not Benoni's wood but a common, a great mixed wood of pine, birch and aspen.

At a certain time in the summer the people of two parishes meet here and hack and hew away to their hearts' content; when they have done and have taken the firewood home the place is left to itself for another year and birds and beasts again have perfect peace. Now and then a Lapp on his way from one parish to another passes through the wood; apart from this there is only Benoni, whose way lies here winter and summer. And Benoni goes wet or dry as it may chance; he is a stout fellow who is not put off by difficulties.

Benoni, he's a fisherman like everybody else on the coast. But in addition to this he carries the mail over the mountain and back again; he makes the trip once a fortnight and gets his little fixed payment for the job. It isn't everybody who has a regular government salary once a quarter, and so Benoni is a great lad and raises some dust among his fellows. Of course now and then somebody would come home from outside after a lucky shot of herring and would walk around whistling loudly by reason of money and consideration. But this was never of long persistence. The worthy fellows were so deep in the books of Trader Mack at Sirilund that when their debts were wiped out there was nothing left for themselves but a memory of the time they went about whistling with opulence. Whereas Benoni unvaryingly,

Benoni

year in, year out, carried the Royal Mail on his back, and he was absolutely a lad and a person of consequence with a lock and a lion on his mail-bag.

One morning he came through the common on his way over the mountain; it was summer and there were a few men about cutting wood. And there was the neighbouring parson's daughter in hat and feathers.

"There's Benoni," she said; "now I'll have someone to see me home." And her name was Rosa.

Benoni bowed and replied that if he might be so bold.

She was a proud lady, Benoni knew her well, had seen her grow up; but now he had seen nothing of her for a year or so, wherever she might have been. And the Arentsens, the parish clerk and his wife, had a son, a bright spark who had been down South for many years acquiring legal learning; so perhaps it was Young Arentsen Rosa went to see when she was away from home. Nobody knew anything for certain, Rosa kept so quiet.

Aye, Rosa had her little secrets too, quite remarkable things, for her own private consumption. As to-day, for instance, she must have made up her mind to start out across country at four in the morning, so as to reach the common by eight. She was plucky enough for that. Her father too was a great man and proud; he spent all his spare time in shooting and every kind of sport. But besides this he had a great gift of speech.

They walked chatting together for an hour or two, Benoni and Rosa, and she asked him a lot of questions. They sat down and rested, Benoni offered her some of his lunch and she did justice to it to show him honour. Then they went on for another hour; rain began to fall, heavy and warm, and Rosa proposed that they should take shelter. But Benoni, who was carrying the Royal Mail, could not spare time for that. They went on walking, till Rosa slipped in the wet and was not so clever at keeping her feet.

Benoni

Benoni looked at her and felt pity for the lady. And he looked up at the sky and guessed that the rain was soon going to stop, and to oblige her he said:

"If so be you would make do with a plain rock to sit under."

They went in under the ledge of rock and found a regular cave.

"Why, we can sit splendidly here," said Rosa, and she crawled a long way in. "Now if one might borrow your bag with the lion on it, Benoni, to sit on."

"I dursn't do that for anything," Benoni answered, shocked. "But if you'd make shift with an old jacket."

With that, Benoni pulled off his jacket and gave it to the lady to sit on.

What a ready fellow he is!—she must have thought for her part, and perhaps she had a good opinion of the young man. She chaffed him and even wanted to know the name of his girl.

After about ten minutes Benoni went out into the open and took another look at the sky. At that moment a vagabond Lapp was passing and saw him. And it was none other than Gilbert the Lapp.

"Is she still raining?" asked Benoni for the sake of saying something. He was a trifle flustered.

"No, she's clear," answered the Lapp.

Benoni fetched his mail-bag and his jacket out of the cave and the parson's daughter followed him.

The Lapp stood and watched. . . .

And Gilbert the Lapp went down to the coast and spread the news abroad, and he went all the way to the store at Sirilund.

"Say, Benoni," people began to twit him after that day, "what were you doing at Holla with Rosa parson's daughter? You came out half naked and warm and you had no coat on. What are we to think of it?"

Benoni

"You're to think that you're an old gossip," replied Benoni in a voice of authority. "Just let me catch the Lapp that's been talking!"

But time wore on and Gilbert the Lapp took courage to meet Benoni again.

"Ah, what were you doing at Holla that time and what took you in there?" he asked cautiously. And he smiled and screwed up his eyes as if he was looking at the sun.

"Never you mind," answered Benoni slyly and smiled back. That was all he did to the Lapp.

Benoni had begun to be a little puffed up over the big rumour that was afloat about himself and Rosa parson's daughter. Christmas came on; as he sat over his Christmas brandy with paltry fellows of his own class he felt he was indeed a man who was raised above them. And now the Sheriff had appointed him writ-server and there wasn't an auction or a distraint that Benoni didn't have to be there. And as he was well skilled in reading and writing he had at a pinch to read out the Sheriff's notices at the church door.

Aye, life was helpful, life was obliging to Benoni, to Post Benoni. And everything he undertook turned out well. Soon Rosa parson's daughter was not a scrap too good for him.

"That day at Holla!" he said with a smack of the lips.

"You don't mean to say it's true that you got at her?" asked his cronies.

Benoni replied:

"Well, maybe you're not far out."

"My word! And now you're going to marry her?"

Benoni replied again:

"Never you mind about that. It depends on that Benoni and me and nobody else."

"But what will that Nikolai Arentsen say to it, eh?"

Benoni

"What can Nikolai say? He's out of it."

So there he had said it.

And it was said so often and by so many people that it must be right. God knows, perhaps Benoni began to believe it himself.

II

WHEN the respected clergyman of the neighbouring parish, the Reverend Jacob Barfod, sent a message to anyone that he wished to see him in his study, there was nothing to do but to go. He had two doors to his study, one outside the other, and as soon as they were through the first one, most men pulled off their caps.

He sent for Benoni the next time he came with the mail.

"This is what I get for my valiant tongue," thought Benoni anxiously. "The parson has heard of my boasting and now he is going to ruin and destroy me." But as he had got the message there was nothing for it but to go. Benoni pulled off his cap between the two doors and walked in.

But there was no danger in the parson to-day. On the contrary, he had a favour to ask of Benoni.

"You see these blue fox-skins," he said. "I have had them since early winter. I can't get rid of them here. Take them with you to Mack at Sirilund."

Benoni was so marvellously relieved that he began to babble:

"Yes, I'll certainly do that. It shall be done this very evening, by six o'clock this evening."

"Tell Mack from me that blue fox is at eight to ten dollars."

Benoni babbled again in his great relief:

"Ten dollars? Say twenty. They shan't go for a song, certainly not."

"And then you will bring me the money, Benoni."

Benoni

"Next trip. As sure as you see me standing here. . . .
I shall lay the money right on your table."

As Benoni went home over the mountain he felt neither
hunger nor weariness from sheer satisfaction with himself
and with life. Look now, the parson had already begun
to make use of him, admitting him in a way as a member
of the family. One day Fröken Rosa would surely take
a step further.

He got ten dollars apiece right enough for the fox-skins
and Benoni brought back the money safe and sound. But
that time the parson was away; he saw the mistress and
had to hand the notes to her. He was given coffee and a
dram for his trouble.

And once more Benoni returned to his cottage on the
coast. He was full of thoughts. Now Fröken Rosa
would have to do something; spring was coming on and
the time had arrived for a decision.

Then he wrote a letter to the parson's daughter and
made a good job of it. He ended by asking her in so
many words not to throw him over altogether. And
yours respectfully Benoni Hartvigsen, writ-server.

He brought the letter himself. . . .

But now life was no longer obliging to Benoni. His
bragging and disgraceful fictions over the Christmas
brandy had at last reached the neighbouring parish and
Rosa parson's daughter. Bad times were coming.

The parson sent for him again. Benoni had dressed
himself smartly and well as he always did of late, with
one jacket over the other so that he could wear the outer
one unbuttoned. And besides that he had a particularly
handsome print shirt.

"This is the answer to my letter," thought Benoni;
"he wants to know my intentions. He may be right;
there's many a base deceiver and seducer in this world,
but I am not like that."

Benoni

Benoni was uneasy. He went first into the parsonage kitchen to get a hint or two if he could; he might find a face that would betray something.

"The parson wanted to see you," said the maids.

Oh, well, at any rate he couldn't get more than a No to his letter. And he'd be just as good a man for all that. He'd never been so specially set on the parson's daughter either.

"All right," he answered, pulling himself together. "I'll go in." And he smoothed back his shock of hair; for he had such a thick and shaggy head of hair.

"He only wants to ask another favour of me," he thought on his way to the study.

Both the parson and his daughter were standing there when he came in. Neither answered his greeting. The parson handed him a paper and said:

"Will you read that?"

Then the parson began to walk up and down the room. Meanwhile Rosa stood by the writing-table, tall and mute.

Benoni read. It was a statement to the effect that I, Benoni Hartvigsen, hereby publicly retract any defamatory inventions I have disseminated about myself and Fröken Rosa Barfod and declare the same to be disgraceful untruths.

Benoni was given plenty of time to read it. At last the parson, irritated by his trembling hands and his long silence, asked:

"Haven't you read it yet?"

"Yes," answered Benoni feebly.

"What do you say to it?"

Benoni faltered:

"I suppose it's all right. I couldn't expect anything else."

And Benoni shook his head.

The parson said:

Benoni

"Sit down here and sign your name to the declaration."

Benoni put his cap on the floor and crept up to the table and signed. He did not forget the long flourish under his name that he had practised of late.

"Now this paper will be sent to the Sheriff in your own parish to be read out at the church door," said the parson.

Benoni's head was so dull and heavy; he answered:

"Yes, I suppose so."

All this time Rosa had been standing by the writing-table, tall and mute. . . .

Life was no longer obliging. It would soon be spring, the crows were beginning to gather twigs; but where was the joy and the singing, the smile and the glory? And what did Benoni care now for the big catch of herrings! He had a small share in three seines that had made a shot; he had thought in his pride that this might have been some comfort to him and Rosa parson's daughter—what a miserable fool he had been!

He kept his bed for a whole day from vexation and saw his old charwoman come and go and come again. And when she asked if he was sick, he was sick, and when she asked if he wasn't better, he obliged her by saying Yes, he was better.

He did not get up the next day either. It was Saturday. A messenger arrived with a packet from the Sheriff.

"Here's a man with a packet from the Sheriff," said the charwoman by his bed.

Benoni replied:

"Ah, well, put the packet there."

It's notices for me to read out to-morrow, thought Benoni. He lay a while longer, then got up suddenly and opened the packet: auctions, escaped prisoners, the annual assessment. And there too lay his own declaration. He grasped his head with both hands.

Benoni

So he was to do it himself, stand by the church door and publish his own disgrace!

He clenched his teeth and said:

"Aye, aye, Benoni!"

But when the morrow came with bright sunshine, he did not read his own declaration. He read everything else and not that; the sun, the sun was too strong and a hundred eyes looked him in the face.

He betook himself home in a state of mournful depression; he avoided company and made his way through wood and bog so as to be alone. Ah, it was the last time Benoni had a chance to refuse company, he was never offered it again.

It soon came out that Benoni had suppressed papers at the church door. Next Sunday the Sheriff put on his gold-laced cap and read the declaration himself in the hearing of a great crowd of people.

An unheard-of thing had befallen the neighbourhood and it buzzed with talk from the beach up to the hills. Benoni had fallen, he handed over the bag with the lion on it and had carried the mail for the last time. Henceforth he was nothing on God's earth.

He went home to his cottage and brooded and fretted for a week. One evening a master-seiner came to his cottage and handed him over his share in a shot of herring. Thanks, said Benoni. The next evening came master-seiner Norum who had made the big shot just off Benoni's house. For this Benoni got his three small shares in the seine and a big royalty into the bargain. Thanks, said Benoni.

It was all the same to him, he was nothing at all now.

III

IF Trader Mack of Sirilund wanted to do a man a good or a bad turn he had the power to do it. And there was both black and white in his soul. He resembled his brother Mack of Rosengaard in that he could do what he liked; but now and then he surpassed him in doing what he ought not to do.

Now Mack sent word to Benoni to appear at Sirilund immediately.

Benoni accompanied the messenger, who was none other than one of Mack's store clerks.

Benoni was frightened of everything on earth and said dejectedly:

"What do you think he wants with me? Did he look ungracious?"

"I couldn't say what he wants with you," said the man.

"Let me go, in God's name!" said Benoni gloomily.

When he stood outside Mack's office he was more cowed and humble than ever. He stood there so long twisting and twirling and pulling himself together that Mack himself heard him and opened the door with a jerk.

"Oh, it's you—come in," said Mack himself.

And nobody could have told whether he meant to raise Benoni up or to hurl him down.

Mack said:

"You have behaved badly."

"Yes," said Benoni.

"But the others have behaved just as badly," said Mack. With that he began to pace up and down the room,

Benoni

stopping at the window and looking out. Suddenly he turned round and asked:

"You've made a heap of money lately?"

"Yes, said Benoni.

"What are you going to do with it?"

"I don't know. I don't care about anything."

"You'll buy herring with it," said Mack. "Here's herring just outside your own door, you'll salt and cure all the herring you can afford and send it South. Barrels and salt you can get from me, if you like."

Some moments passed and Benoni made no sound, till Mack asked curtly:

"Well, will you begin to-morrow?"

"As you say," answered Benoni.

Mack went to the window again and turned his back; he must have been thinking. Oh, that Mack was a great man for thinking! Benoni was given a little time to himself and began to think too. Mack was a slippery devil in business, perhaps his soul was more black than white. Benoni knew that Mack owned the greater part of the herring that had been caught outside his cottage; now he wanted to seize the opportunity of getting rid of some of it, selling high. It was already late in the season and the herring was not in the best condition. Besides which he would find a customer for some of his big stock of empty barrels and salt.

Benoni thought over all this and said:

"Well, it depends on the price. That's understood."

"I'm going to help you on," said Mack, turning round. "You must get started again with something. You've done wrong, but so have the others, and this lesson ought to be enough."

You'll see, he means it, thought Benoni. He felt all at once mild and grateful and said:

"I am greatly beholden to you."

Benoni

Then Mack spoke like the mighty man he was and said:
"I mean to send a little note to our good neighbour the pastor. For that matter, I am Rosa's godfather; I shall let her and her father know one or two things from me. Well, you needn't know anything about that. How much money have you?"

"Oh, it may come to a bit altogether."

"You understand, of course," said Mack, "that your dollars are of no particular consequence to me. I assume you're quite clear about that. So it's not for that. What I want is to set you on your feet again."

"All thanks and honour to you for it."

"You spoke about the price. We can talk about that to-morrow. We'll meet on board the seining-boat."

Mack nodded in sign that that was all; but when Benoni had reached the door he called out:

"Oh, look here, as I mentioned that about the letter, here it is. You can go inside and put it in the post, then it will be sent to-morrow." . . .

Benoni became a buyer of herring. He had people under him who gutted and salted his herring and rolled his barrels up and down. If Mack of Sirilund had shown renewed confidence in him, who could be so presumptuous as to hold back? In the end Benoni had some of the old joyful feeling of prosperity in his powerful chest.

He had by no means allowed himself to be led into a fool's bargain by Trader Mack. This first little encouragement had made him the quick and sensible lad again and he did not put all his money into herrings. Half would have to do, thought Benoni. Besides, Mack's letter to the reverend Barfod was now sent off and Mack could not take it back again.

Benoni bought herrings and salted herrings and began to be something of a man again. He noticed now that folks had taken to touching their hats to him when he passed and

Benoni

that they spoke respectfully to him because he had become a trader in their midst.

His herring deal might easily have turned out badly and Mack himself scarcely made the fortune he had expected in the beginning. But while Mack went into it on a large scale and sent two cargo steamers to Bergen with his herrings in bulk, Benoni in modest style chartered one of Mack's sloops and sailed her south himself with a couple of hands at the end of the spring. He put in at big places and small and sold his goods a barrel at a time. He might have done worse, he made a little, put money by. He was home again by midsummer.

Then it was that Rosa parson's daughter crossed his path again; he met her at church, she was on horseback. It was a rare thing to see anyone riding thereabouts and all the church-goers regarded her with curiosity. Benoni took off his hat with a humble and modest bow and got her to nod. There was not a shadow to be seen on her face; she rode off at a walk and the wind carried her veil back like a long streak of blue smoke. She was like a vision.

Once more Benoni made his way home from church through bogs and woods. I am more miserable than many other creatures, he thought, but maybe the fine lady has heard that I am on my feet again and getting on in a small way. What else should she nod for?

Late in the summer he got an offer to sail Mack's dried fish to Bergen in the schooner. He had never been to Bergen before, but everything must have a beginning; if others could find the way there, he could find it too.

"I see you have a good hand at all kinds of things," were Mack's words to him.

"I have such hands and feet as you have given me back," answered Benoni with perfect correctness, giving Mack the honour.

Benoni

It was no small step to be made skipper of the schooner *Funtus;* Benoni now ranked at least with the schoolteachers round about, and, being a man of money, he had no need to step aside and let the small outlying traders pass.

He was home again with the schooner some time before Christmas; all had gone well and his vessel was laden with all kinds of goods which Mack got from Bergen in this way to save freight.

Benoni was like an admiral at heart as he came ashore and acknowledged the greetings of the people on the quay. Mack received him well and nobly and gave him a drink in his own private parlour. It was the first time Benoni had been there, and there were big pictures on the walls and gilt furniture that had been handed down from father to son, and there was a chandelier hanging from the ceiling with hundreds of drops of pure crystal. After that they went into the office, where Benoni produced his accounts and Mack thanked him.

Now indeed Benoni's reputation stood higher than ever, and after a while, led by Mack himself, people began to call him Hartvigsen. Not even in the days when he was the King's postman and writ-server had he been Hartvigsen to a mother's son of them, but now he was. He provided curtains for the windows of his cottage, though this was perhaps going rather too far, and there was some comment about it at the parish clerk's. He had brought back some fine white shirts from Bergen and wore them when he went to church. . . .

At Christmas time he was invited to Mack's house. Mack was now left alone, his daughter Edvarda was married to a Finnish Baron and never came home any more; a strange housekeeper had charge of everything, but she was a practised hand and fond of company.

There were several guests and Rosa parson's daughter

Benoni

was there. When Benoni saw her he sidled off shyly to the wall.

Mack said:

"This is Fröken Barfod, you know her. She is not one to bear a grudge."

"My Godfather tells me you are innocent, Benoni," said Rosa straight out. "That you were keeping Christmas and it was someone else who said it. That alters the case."

"I don't know . . . maybe I myself . . . didn't say it," mumbled Benoni.

"We're not going to hear another word about that affair," said Mack, and he led away Rosa like a father.

Benoni felt better, a load was taken off him, a light appeared, Mack had helped him again, aye, cleansed him to the whiteness of wool. He felt man enough to go up and speak to the Sheriff. Afterwards, at table, he may not have behaved in every way like the other gentlemen, but he kept a good eye on them and learnt one or two things that evening. Mack's housekeeper sat next him and was a good hostess.

From the talk at table he heard that Rosa parson's daughter was going away again for a short trip. He looked at her on the quiet. To be proud and grand was to be proud and grand, there was nothing else about it. It was no use making money out of herrings and putting up curtains in your rooms; if you were not born to greatness you went on being Benoni. Rosa must be past her first youth, but she had a wealth of light-brown hair and she laughed heartily and handsomely with her ripe mouth. And there was nobody so full-bosomed as she. I'll see I'm not such a fool as to look at her any more, thought Benoni.

"They've already been taking some herring in the fiords," said Mack to him on the quiet, showing him an express message. "Come to the office early to-morrow."

Benoni

Benoni would rather have stayed at home awhile to enjoy the consideration that his command of the schooner brought him. But all the same he went to Mack in the morning.

"I have an offer to make you," said Mack. "I'll make over my big seine to you for cash, so you can work your own seine. As I said, they're taking herring in the fiords."

Benoni was not lacking in gratitude and he thought of the help Mack had lent him the night before. But the big seine had seen its best days. He said simply:

"But I'm not up to that."

"You are, you are," replied Mack. "You have a lucky hand. It's different with me, I have to have others to do everything and I have nobody to work the seine."

"I'd rather try and work it for you," Benoni offered.

Mack shook his head and said:

"You shall have it cheap, with boats and windlass, and two pairs of binoculars thrown in. You shall have it dirt-cheap."

"I'll think about it," Benoni answered with a heavy heart.

He thought and thought, but the end of it was that he bought the seine. There was none like Mack and he couldn't afford to do without his favour. He got a crew together and sailed into the fiords with the big seine.

Now there was nothing for it but the mercy of Heaven!

He lay for three weeks in company with other seiners and kept a look-out. There was no herring to speak of; he made a few casts, but only got enough for the men's suppers, and his big seine cost too much for that. His spirits grew gloomier and gloomier, the greater part of his wealth now lay in a seine that was half worn out and earning nothing but simply getting more rotten every day. Mack's help after all had cost nim dear.

One evening he said to his crew:

Benoni

"There's nothing to be done here. We'll warp out again to-night."

They went off in silence, warping and sailing. The night was raw and cold, they kept along the coast. It drew on towards morning. Benoni was on the point of leaving the helm in disgust and turning in, when he heard a distant murmur from seaward. He looked to the east and he looked to the west in the darkness, but saw no sign of storm. What a queer hum there is in the air! thought Benoni. He stayed at the helm, steering along the coast with the sea on his beam; it grew a little lighter, a misty dawn. Now the strange hum in the air came nearer. Suddenly Benoni jumped up and took his glasses; there was not much to be seen yet, but now he knew from the distant birds' cries what was coming. He instantly turned out his crew and set them to work.

It was the herring coming from seaward.

With an immense school of whales and a whirling, shrieking tumult of birds the herring were being chased into the fiords.

Benoni's boats were too far out of the way, almost inshore, and before he had time to sail into the middle of the fiord the whales and birds had passed him. The sea was white with foam and sea-birds.

"We shouldn't have sailed out," thought Benoni gloomily.

There was nothing to be done now but to beat back into the fiord, hour after hour, and possibly arrive at the end of the feast.

It grew light. Now and then a belated whale rushed past.

Then Benoni saw the great army of birds returning from inside the fiord and meeting him again; the herring had made a great sweep round and the whales were still chasing them. Benoni found himself outside a creek in

Benoni

the coast-line; something or other had happened to make the mass of herring divide into two shoals, a confusion had arisen, perhaps it was the belated whales meeting the stream and cleaving it. The herring flashed like hosts of stars round Benoni's boats. It was no use shooting the seine with all those whales about; Benoni stood with his heart in his mouth. Then he saw that the whole creek was boiling and the air above it white with birds, the creek was bursting with herring. Benoni called out an order, short and sharp, and lent a hand here and there; the seine ran out. It was stretched right across the creek from one shore to the other, the herring were packed up against the dry land. Here the big seine was the only thing.

A tremendous noise of whales and birds still came from seaward, showing the way the other shoal had gone.

Benoni was dripping with sweat and his knees shook as he got into the dinghy. He had himself rowed along the seine to see if it stood true and taut.

"It was a good thing we sailed out after all," he thought.

He sent off two men with a letter to Mack of Sirilund to tell him of his great shot. He reported the quality of the herring, that it was a good mixture; the depth of the creek, that there was no risk of a taste of the ground. Further he reported that it was like the finger of God: the herring had turned inside the fiord and come and shut themselves up in a creek right before his eyes. . . . "As regards the size of the shot I will not make bold to put a figure to it which He alone who counts the stars of heaven can reckon up. But it is very big. Respectfully, Benoni Hartvigsen, my name."

Mack, as ever, was a good friend to him and sent off expresses east and west of his own accord to find buyers for Benoni. And every day sailers and steamers glided into the fiord and lay outside Benoni's seine; fishing-

Benoni

boats came too from his own district to get bait herring for the Lofoten fishery and with them he kept no strict account, but gave them cran after cran for nothing.

Now there was such traffic as had never been known before in the quiet creek, travelling traders and Jew pedlars and rope-dancers and loose women from the towns, it was like a fair; a regular little town of tents and booths and packing-cases arose on the naked shores. And money gleamed like herring-scales in everybody's hand. . . .

IV

MACK himself said to Benoni in the spring:
"I'll tell you what, my good Hartvigsen, you ought to get married."

On hearing this, Benoni put on an air of deep humility and answered:

"There's nobody who will have me."

"But of course you must marry according to your rank and means and not throw yourself away," Mack continued unperturbed. "I know of a certain lady. Well, we won't talk about that. Tell me, Hartvigsen, have you lost very much in your dealings with me so far in this world?"

"Lost?"

"It looks so strange. You must have a lot of money; but you don't deposit it with me."

"It's no great means that I have."

"So you keep it in a stocking? That is so curious. Your forefathers used to keep their money with mine, and so you should keep yours with me. I mention it for no other reason than that it's what we are all accustomed to."

Benoni answered hesitatingly:

"It's like this, you see, old folks have given me such a scare."

"Ah? They must have been telling you about the failures after the war? My father was a great business man and he didn't go bankrupt. I am no mean business man either and I am not bankrupt. That is, I hope to God I'm not."

"I had been thinking of coming to you with my poor mite," said Benoni.

Benoni

Then Mack wandered back to the window and began to think as was his habit; his back was turned to Benoni. He was inclined to be chatty:

"They come to me from all the country round and I'm like a father to them. They give me their small cash till they want it again and I give them a receipt with my name to it: Sirilund, such and such a date, Ferdinand Mack. Then after a time, short or long as it may be, they come back and ask for their money; and here's the receipt, they say. Good, I count out the money, here you are! Then they say: But this is too much, it wasn't so much as this. That's the interest, I tell them."

"Aye, the interest," said Benoni in spite of himself.

"Of course there's interest. I use money and I make money," answered Mack, turning from the window. "And as regards you, Hartvigsen, yours is a considerable sum, you see. I shan't give you a simple receipt but a solemn bond, a mortgage. I'm not saying it for any other reason, but that's what I shall do. Big capitalists can't be treated like little ones, they must have security. For, you see, your sum is not one that I can take out of my waistcoat pocket and hand back to you any day, so you shall have a mortgage on Sirilund and its appurtenances and on the vessels."

"You're monkeying!" exclaimed Benoni in bewilderment. Then he corrected the disrespectful phrase and added: "I mean you ought not to say such things. It's going too far altogether."

From a child Benoni had never heard but one opinion of the greatness of Mack of Sirilund. The trading-station alone with its quays, its mills, spirit license, steamer pier, bake-house and smithy was worth his little fortune many times over; and then there was the estate with its bird rocks for eggs, its bogs for cloudberries and its drying grounds for fish; lastly the schooner and the two sloops.

Benoni

Mack met Benoni's bewilderment with a gently patronizing air:

"All I say is that that is my way of doing things. To that extent you could feel that your money was safe. But we won't speak any more about it."

Benoni stammered:

"Oh, but please let me have a little time to think about it. If I hadn't been so scared by old folks . . . But if you . . . I've a good mind to do it."

"We won't say another word about it. Do you know what I was thinking about just now at the window? My goddaughter, Fröken Rosa Barfod. She just came into my mind. Have you thought about her at all, Hartvigsen? Young people are strange creatures; she went South after Christmas and was to have been away a year, but now she's come home again. Perhaps there's some attraction here. Well, good-bye, Hartvigsen. You can think over what I said about the money, if you like. Just as you like." . . .

But now it so happened that the good Benoni let one day after another go by without falling in with Mack's suggestion about the money. Let him take his time, thought Mack of Sirilund, that slippery eel in all matters of business; let him keep back his answer for the present, he must have thought. For he didn't even take the trouble to send for Benoni.

Benoni was not lacking in brains, and Mack's hint about Rosa parson's daughter had not escaped him. When he had pondered night and day and grown smarter and smarter he formed a resolution to go past Mack and act for himself. No, he was nothing like the great master of wealth that Mack tried to make him out; where should he have got it? Ho-ho, Benoni had not been a sharp lad for nothing.

He dressed himself finely in two jackets and a church-

Benoni

going shirt and started across the common and over the mountain. He steered straight for the parsonage. He had calculated beforehand that Pastor Barfod would be away at the chapel of ease.

He went into the kitchen and gave out that business had brought him this way, he had to cross the sound. Did they think the parson would lend him his boat?

The parson was away, answered the maids.

But wasn't the mistress or Fröken Rosa at home? Just say it's Benoni Hartvigsen.

He got the boat. But neither the mistress nor Rosa came out and said Good day, good day, Hartvigsen; won't you come in?

It's no good! thought Benoni. He rowed across the sound, strolled about the woods for some time, rowed back and went once more into the parsonage kitchen to return thanks for the boat.

The same thing over again, not a glimpse of the family.

It's no good at all! thought Benoni on his way home over the mountain. He was tough as steel in many ways, but in dealing with the gentry he lost his spirit altogether. What am I to do? he asked, still thinking of Rosa. Shall I marry according to my affluence, or shall I marry one of my former equals and sink into nothing?

He gave himself a great deal to do at home; he now had four carpenters building a big boat-house for the seine outfit. But his spirits were no brighter for all that; his dissatisfaction increased, he grew suspicious, it seemed to him that people had taken to calling him Benoni again instead of Hartvigsen.

Wherein had he deserved this ignominy?

One day Mack said to him:

"You are building a boat-house, you needn't have done that. I would have let you have free storage for the seine as before. On the other hand, there is something else you

Benoni

might build—you ought to add to your cottage. If you are to marry as befits your means, you must have a couple of rooms more. The ladies expect it."

They talked about this at some length and suddenly it occurred to Benoni that the least he could do was to show confidence in Mack and go and fetch his money. On his way home he weighed it all again: with the mighty security that Mack put up, his cash was in no danger; on the contrary, it made him Mack's secret partner and part-owner of Sirilund. Ah, money, if luck went with it, it made a beggar into a lord.

He came with his riches in a sack, a great lot of silver; Benoni wouldn't be the man to skimp the amount; if Mack had formed such a big opinion of him as a rich man, he would by no means prove him wrong. So he scraped together exactly five thousand specie-dollars to make a mighty round sum.

And sure enough, "My goodness!" said Mack to flatter him.

"You must excuse my humble purse. I haven't a better," Benoni remarked pompously.

Mack wouldn't give him any more rope.

"But all this silver!" he said. "Why, notes are now at par."

"What are they at?"

"Par. That means they are every bit as good as silver. You know that, don't you? Well, silver's good enough."

"I thought it was pretty good money I was bringing you, silver or paper," said Benoni, rather hurt.

Again Mack wouldn't allow his pride any more rope, he pulled him up short: "Of course!" and began to count. It took a long time, the dollars were stacked into piles which were tumbled into heaps and then swept into a bag. Then the notes were counted, and then Mack with true solemnity went to work and wrote out a big bond.

Benoni

"You must take great care of this document," he told Benoni significantly. . . .

But now another very great event took place: Rosa parson's daughter not only came on a visit to Sirilund but positively began to look Benoni in the face with kind and thoughtful eyes as though she were considering him. One day she came down to the beach and said:

"I just want to see your new boat-house."

"It's no great thing for you to look at," Benoni replied in his first joyful confusion. Presently, when he had recovered a little, he said: "I am going to build on to the cottage too."

"Fancy! How much are you adding?"

"I thought of another parlour and bedroom," Benoni answered cautiously.

"That's quite right," said Fröken Rosa kindly. "So then you're going to be married?"

"Well, that's as may be."

"You see, I don't know how she will think about it, but if I were in your place I should make that bedroom pretty big and light."

"Yes," said Benoni. "Is that how you would like it?"

"Yes."

Benoni grew bold before she left him and said:

"If it's not asking too much, you must come and see it when it's finished."

So Benoni built the parlour and the big bedroom and he exaggerated a little and made the bedroom just as big as the parlour. When Rosa saw it, his heart was in his boots for fear it might not be right. But again she said kindly that that was what she had meant.

Now just here on the spot he might have said a word, but he didn't say it. He went over to Mack that evening and asked him to say it—that is, if he thought there was any possible chance.

Benoni

Mack delivered his message in a few straight words, smiled a little at them both and left the room.

There they sat alone.

"I must tell you, Benoni, that I don't think this will bring you any joy," said Rosa frankly. "I have been engaged for a long time to a man down South: it was not for nothing I was away from home so much."

"Then perhaps you are to marry him, possibly?"

"No, it won't come to anything. It will never come to anything with him."

"Well, if so be you would put up with me? But I'm not any different than what you see me, a plain man. So it's not to be expected."

Rosa thought and blinked her eyes slowly.

"We might try it, Benoni. My godfather thinks I ought to do it. But I must tell you," she added, smiling, "that you are not my first love."

"No, no, that I can't expect. But I'm not troubling about that," replied Benoni in his play-acting manner.

So they were agreed. . . .

During the weeks that followed, there was much talk about this singular occurrence, which may have been a dispensation of Providence, but was strange enough for all that. But at the parish clerk's they said straight out: "Dispensation of Providence? It's the herring that's done it. If that Benoni hadn't grown so fabulously rich on herrings he would never have got her."

For you see, there was that son of the parish clerk's who would have been a far better match for Rosa parson's daughter.

V

SO some weeks went by; Rosa often came to see Mack at Sirilund and each time Benoni met her. People didn't tease them about it; it was not their way to chaff a couple who denied nothing, and Rosa and Post Benoni, they openly admitted it all and said Yes, they were going to be married.

Benoni went on fitting up his house and his boat-shed; he was now panelling and painting his home like other people of importance, and men who saw it from the sea would say: "There's that Benoni's mansion."

Sirilund had a veranda and Benoni took it into his head that he would have one like it, on a small scale of course, without any carving, just a sort of place to sit with a couple of seats. He spoke about it first to one of the painters.

"I'm getting so grand that I want to put up a shed here," he said; "just a paltry lean-to," he said.

The painter, a local man, couldn't see. A shed?

"Folks call it a veranda," said Benoni, turning away.

"What do you want with it?"

"No, I dare say you're quite right there. It's only to pass the time, to have a place to stand and look out."

Was the painter laughing? Benoni settled it there and then; he was not going to stand any sniggering in his face. He called up the carpenters, explained what he wanted with unnecessary clearness, gave them the height, pointed.

"It's to be a place to sit and drink coffee in the summertime," he said.

Benoni

The carpenters were quicker at taking him up, they came from outside and had seen a great deal of the world.

"People with the means for it have verandas," said the carpenters and nodded.

A few days later Benoni got another idea in his head. There was likewise a dovecote at Sirilund. It stood in the middle of the yard on a single post, it was painted white and had a brass ball on top. There was some life in those birds, and chickens were not in it with doves.

"If so be I got some real doves one day I shouldn't know where to put them," said Benoni.

He took the carpenters with him and showed them where the dovecote was to stand.

And the weeks went by, autumn came, Benoni was busy at home and did not go out with the seine. The carpenters and painters had gone; their last exploit was to put coloured glass in the veranda so that it looked like the entrance to a paradise. Not even Sirilund had coloured glass in its veranda, that bright lad Benoni had invented it out of his own head. There were panes of blue, red and yellow glass.

But when the workmen were gone Benoni found it slow; he went to Rosa and said it was no life to be leading for a lone person, and what did she think about changing her state? But Rosa, she was in no hurry to give herself away, they might be married in the spring, there was time enough.

Meanwhile Benoni did a little inshore fishing; but when the bay began to freeze over, it was too much trouble to break a passage through and the fishing came to an end. Then Benoni had nothing in the world to do but go to church on Sundays. Oh, there were days when he could have wished he was carrying the bag with the lion on it again; but now it was carried by one of the parson's tenants, a breadwinner of no consideration.

Benoni

There was Benoni Hartvigsen on his way to church. He had on two jackets and sea-boots with glazed tops. Not a sign of a stoop in his back, he walked straight as a monument, and when he sang the hymns there was no shirking about it. If he talked to folks outside the church he was not like a fool who refused to recognize the small people of the place; but he didn't hang about and get cold for the sake of a chat. "That Mack and I!" he would say. "You may believe me, we got an express yesterday, the herring's coming in from sea!" When the Sheriff's officer had read out his notices he came up and put a few questions: The herring—was there any news from outside? Benoni answered: "That Mack and I were aboard the steamer yesterday to find out." One more question and Benoni announced: "From to-morrow I shall begin to get busy!"

The populace stood around and nodded: a deuce of a fellow Benoni, he got word from the Almighty Himself, or next thing to it, when there was herring about! And Benoni pushed his hand through his shock of hair and smiled with his strong, yellow walrus teeth: No, that was saying a bit too much, that was exaggerating; but he did know a thing or two in his humble way.

The Sheriff's officer joined him as they left the church. The two might rank more or less as equals; Benoni had his great wealth but the other was admittedly superior in his talk and manners. And it was only when Benoni had ceased to be writ-server and the Sheriff's right hand that the old man had been obliged to get this officer from town.

They talked about Benoni's house, about his veranda, which was grand, about the dovecote, the wedding. Benoni spoke with patronizing banter of womenfolk, the fair sex; could any man on earth make out what was in their heads? What did he want with him, who was nothing

Benoni

but a poor master of a schooner! And he called Rosa his sweetheart.

"I'll venture to say," said the Sheriff's officer, "that you wouldn't let her go for something?"

"Not for all that you see before you," replied Benoni, pointing to his home. "Let her go? There's no such thing; I've won her heart."

"When you and she take a walk and talk together, do you go and talk like we do, about any little thing that comes into your head?"

"I talk to her absolutely just as simply and ignorantly as I talk to you," answered Benoni.

"I never heard the like!" said the Sheriff's officer.

They had reached Benoni's house and the two went in. After a few drams there was food and coffee and more drams; Benoni wanted to overwhelm this guest with hospitality, this equal whom he had got hold of at last, and their chatter filled the room. The Sheriff's officer was a young man in fine clothes and a starched collar; they said he spent his time at the Sheriff's in deep study of all the laws, so he was an awkward one to tackle.

"I'm pretty well up now in all that concerns a lot of things and I've got all the registers at the office in my head," he said. "But Rosa Barfod, or, as I may say, Fröken Rosa Barfod, I don't know that she's one I'd be bold to have any talk with."

"She wouldn't bite you," answered Benoni. "Have any talk with? My dear man, I take her in my arms and lift her. It only wants a bit of dash. But, you understand, I have to be on my good behaviour with a lady like that and put her down again nicely. And I mustn't talk indelicate either or act the swine when she's there. Now here's a tobacco pouch she's given me."

They examined the pouch, which was made of silk and

Benoni

beads. But there Benoni was indulging his fancy to the full, for he had simply bought it in Bergen on his trip with the schooner.

As the pouch was a success, Benoni was fired to indulge his fancy yet further in order to show what kind of a sweetheart he had.

"If I could spare the time to show you all the things she's given me!" he said. "There's collars and ties and handkerchiefs, all in beads and silk. I have drawers and chests full."

"I never heard the like!" said the Sheriff's officer.

Benoni went on:

"You talk about learning and suchlike. But what would you think of one that's learnt more than either of us? She frightened me one time."

"How was that?"

Benoni called to mind an incident that had made a strong impression on him, but he was in no hurry to tell it. He filled the glasses, they drank. Benoni sat with a solemn and mysterious air. It was about a message from the sea. A bottle had been found adrift with a note in it; three men in an eight-oared boat came sailing in from the outer skerries with the bottle. They went to the schoolmaster; he didn't understand a word. They went to the parson; he didn't understand a word. So they took it into their heads to go to Mack with it. . . . "Now you know, there's not many things in this world that Mack doesn't know about; but here he was stuck. I myself was sitting on the sofa in his own parlour when the bottle came and Mack, he began to read. What can this mean? he said. Then he asked me, and I could give no answer. Mack pondered and read and stared at the thing in his hand. Then I began to think there must be something in the note that Mack wanted to keep to himself. It's about herring, I thought, about big fishing outside. For you know yourself, Mack's a great fellow for thinking. But I did him wrong there; all at once he shouted upstairs: 'Rosa!' And Rosa, she came down."

Pause. The two men sat there absorbed in the story. The Sheriff's officer asked:

"She managed it? I can guess quite well how it was, I'm not so stupid as all that: she understood the message?"

Benoni thought and looked important for a good while.

"She understood it!" he said weightily.

"You don't say so!"

"It was just like one of the ten commandments or any other little thing to her."

"I never heard the like!" said the Sheriff's officer.

"It was just like her mother tongue. It gave me the creeps. A little more and I'd have thought she belonged to another world, one of the fairies."

"What was there on the paper?"

"It was about a ship in distress."

They drank a few real good goes after this gruesome tale and forgot the message from the sea. They began to talk about the seine, the schooner *Funtus* and the trip to Bergen.

"Talking about herrings," said Benoni, "I ask nothing better than to make another haul. It's this way with a seine full of herring, it draws a regular little town, it fetches Jew pedlars and goldsmiths, just like a fair. Here am I now, I can't get our gold rings bought until there's herring. I'm helpless with my two empty hands."

But Benoni had kept his best card to the last: Mack's document for the five thousand dollars, the bond. He had no objection to the news' getting out, and on the pretext of having an expert examine the paper he produced it and spread it out before the Sheriff's officer.

Long silence and profound study.

"What do you think of it?" asked Benoni.

Benoni

The Sheriff's officer answered:

"Just as good as gold."

"Yes, that's what I thought. And now is it your opinion that Sirilund with all possible appurtenances is worth those five thousand dollars?" Then Benoni enumerated all these appurtenances, of which he was now actually part-owner. He was bursting with importance.

The Sheriff's officer continued to scrutinize the paper and finally said:

"But it must be registered. That is the law."

VI

THE herring Benoni had prophesied did not come and he had no chance of buying the gold rings. It was not as it should be. Benoni went to Sirilund and said to Rosa:

"What do you think about changing our state?" As she did not answer: Yes, let us! but put on a closed and negative look, he asked: "Can't we put up the banns anyhow?"

"There's plenty of time," she answered. "Are you not going to Lofoten this winter?"

"I haven't thought of it."

He was a little huffed. A man in his position did not go out fishing. She saw too where she had made a mistake and began to beat a retreat:

"I thought you were to have Mack's schooner."

"No. Mack hasn't said anything to me."

"No. And I suppose you won't say anything to him?"

More and more huffed, Benoni answered:

"I'm not so hard up."

She laid her hand on his to make him good again. Ah, that woman, there she sat with her lovely thick lips and wouldn't say: Come and let's get married on the spot! Who could understand the fair sex?

He took her round the neck and kissed her. And she let him do it. That was the second time.

"I'm going to buy you a gold ring and a gold cross," he said.

"Oh, yes. But there's no hurry."

Benoni

"What in the world's the matter with you?" he asked, looking at her. "There's no hurry about anything?"

Her grey eyes began to fade, like a sunset. She got up and moved a few steps away:

"Nothing's the matter with me. . . . Won't there be any herring this year, do you think?"

"That's as may be. But if there's herring I shall go. I reckon that's what you want."

The same over again; she set to work to coax him once more. When he awoke to the fact that these tactics paid, he sulked at suitable intervals and got her to wheedle him back with soft words and pats on the arm. She was so grudging of her advances; she never showed any affection unless he forced it out of her.

"But fix a date," said Benoni. "We must have a date for our wedding."

As she could not get out of it, she did her best to stretch the time and talked of a year or so: what did he think of a year from next Christmas?

Another insult.

"I won't go down on my knees," said Benoni.

Finally they agreed to yield a little on both sides and Rosa threw out a date well on in the next year, a day near midsummer. That meant a good half-year to wait yet; well, nearly seven months. . . .

Before going home, Benoni strolled into Mack's store. Mack himself and his two clerks were putting prices on the new goods that had arrived for Christmas. There were big cases standing open, and from them they filled the shelves with rolls of cloths and things. It was horribly cold in the shop, the ink had frozen to a pulp which Mack thawed with his breath every time he had to write a figure. He had gloves on, but the two clerks worked with bare hands.

A customer or two came and went in the store.

Benoni

Benoni asked for the new almanac. He looked at it, took note of the eclipses and the dates of the Nordland fairs and put a mark far on in the year, round about midsummer. It's a Wednesday, he thought, Sylverius' Day, just on the new moon.

"Is there to be no herring for us this year?" said Mack, adapting himself to Benoni's interests.

Although Mack was so greatly in his debt, Benoni was still flattered to have a friendly word from him, so great was the respect that surrounded the old magnate. Ah, that Mack of Sirilund, he still wore his diamond pin in the front of his fine soft shirt and his feet were shod in expensive town shoes with pointed toes. For many years he had dyed his hair and beard.

"Herring don't exist," said Benoni. "What I'm saying is, could I have a word with you in the office?"

"In a moment."

Did Mack want to gain time, a few minutes for reflection? He had a trick of answering like that. . . . He went on writing tickets for his goods and marking them off on the long invoice from the wholesale house. He had started on a new line, but suddenly broke off when he had thought enough.

"Now I'm at your service," he said, and led the way to the office.

"You mustn't take it ill," Benoni began; "they say I must have the mortgage registered."

"Registered? Why?"

"Because it's the law."

"Who says so?"

"It was somebody. I don't know. They say so."

Mack's expression had changed, but then he said coldly and curtly:

"Very well, register it. What have I to do with it?"

"No offence, but there's this, that it costs some money."

Benoni

"A trifle. I'll pay the fee."

"Well, thanks, that was all I wanted to know. And that it was with your consent."

Contrary to his habit, Mack answered too hastily:

"No, it isn't; it's not with my consent at all. But I must put up with it. H'm. If I hadn't already sent the money south, you should have had it back."

Benoni felt uncomfortable and faltered:

"But please . . . they say . . ."

"Oh, let people say what they like. Isn't my signature on the bond: Sirilund and the date, Ferdinand Mack? I tell you, Hartvigsen, I object to having everybody sticking his nose into my affairs. It's a thing I've never cared for."

"But they say the document must be registered," Benoni kept on. He had noticed the change in Mack's expression and had grown wary all at once.

Mack went to the window and thought. Then he said:

"Good. Give me the paper and I'll see to the registering myself."

"I haven't it on me."

"Then bring it one of these days."

And Mack nodded. That was the sign that negotiations were at an end.

As Benoni walked home he thought, wily and sharp: I wonder why Mack made all that fuss about registering? For people knew that he accepted money on all sides, they brought him their money themselves and deposited it with him when they had a few small savings.

VII

HE had been at home about half an hour when one of Mack's store clerks entered his cottage. And it was Martin the store clerk. He said:
"Mack asks you to come back to the office."
"Why? What does he want with me?"
"I couldn't say. He was talking to Rosa from the parsonage."
"To Rosa? Why, she's my sweetheart, Martin. Why do you call her Rosa from the parsonage to me?"
The clerk was a little sheepish at that.
"What were they talking about?"
"I couldn't say. They mentioned the schooner. That you were to go to Lofoten with the schooner and buy fish."
Pause.
"I'll come," said Benoni.
"And then I was to ask you to bring a receipt."
When Benoni was alone he sat down to consider. Was Rosa absolutely set on having him away? He couldn't make out why. And should he take over the schooner again? To be sure, it wasn't much fun for a lone man to be at home in the long winter weeks; besides, it would give him a chance of coming out into the world and buying that piece of jewellery, the gold ring, that was causing him so much bother.

It was already dusk, Benoni lit a candle, looked out the mortgage and put it in his pocket. As he was about to blow out the candle, he took the paper out of his pocket

Benoni

again and read it through. It was right and correct in every way and there wasn't the most harmless mistake in the whole big sheet. But a receipt was not a thing that one gave up? A receipt was a thing to keep!

He laid the paper back in its safe place in the chest, put out the light and went to Sirilund.

In the dusky passage leading to the store, he came upon Mack having a quiet word with one of his own servant girls. Ah, that gay old rip, he hadn't changed much, wild and greedy-eyed as ever in the dark.

"Come along, Hartvigsen," he commanded, and led the way to the office. . . . "I forgot when you were here to-day . . . I had a feeling I had forgotten something . . . It was the schooner; can you take her this year?"

They talked on about it; there was still no news of herring, so Benoni would miss nothing if he made the trip to Lofoten in the old *Funtus*.

"Don't you want her yourself?"

"I would rather see her in your hands. And you must also undertake the buying of cargo for the sloops. For I can trust you with as many thousands as I like."

Benoni was both proud and touched; once more he was to be admiral in the *Funtus*. He had sailed her through the West Fiord, Folden Fiord and Hustadvik, he could quite well take her to Lofoten. And as to buying fish, why, he had none of Mack's off-hand way of doing business, he often bought cheaper than other men because he looked after the halfpence and was tough at driving a bargain. Yes, he'd try and risk it if Mack had a mind to it. Then they talked about his wages.

As Benoni was going, Mack said:

"By the way, have you the bond with you?"

"I forgot it. What do you think of that? I just had it in my mind, too."

Benoni

"Well, bring it another time when you're coming." ...

From now on, Benoni had something to do and he made preparations for the Lofoten trip as though for a voyage round the world. Every time the weather turned a little milder, he found a pretext for going out to the *Funtus,* which lay pitching in the bay, black and frightfully ugly, but big enough for a North Sea boat. What were the two sloops beside the *Funtus!* They lay there alongside the schooner like nothing at all, laden to the waterline with herrings. And the herrings were to go to Lofoten, when there was a shortage of bait for long-line fishing. But the two sloops were held in such poor estimation that Villads the wharfinger was in charge of one and Man Ole of the other.

Benoni stalked about the *Funtus's* deck, looked up into the rigging and looked out at the weather as if he were already under sail; examined his compass and his chart, tallowed the stays, cleaned up the cabin. And why was it he only appeared on board in mild weather? That devil of a Benoni had an object in it, a prodigiously sly design in it: you see, his new yellow oilskins were useless on frosty days when they stiffened and cracked, but those same oilskins looked fine on the deck of a ship when the frost gave; aye, then they showed up rich and golden in the bay and caught the eye from the windows of Sirilund. ...

"Why do you want to get me away?" said Benoni to Rosa.

"I want to get you away!" she replied. "What are you talking about?"

"It looks like that to me."

She talked him round again and there was peace once more. She said she would have gone home to the parsonage, but that Mack had asked her to stay and help in the store when the big Christmas shopping began. She also told him that she had asked Mack to apply to Benoni for his help.

"He hasn't spoken about it."

"But he'll do so to-day. . . . So now you see that I don't want you away from me."

Benoni quivered like a youth at this kindness and put his arms around her. This was the third time he had kissed her and nothing could make it less. "You're just like taking hold of a flower," he said.

Sure enough, Mack requested him to lend a hand during the busy time before Christmas. He need not do more than he liked, he was only to be there and keep an eye on things and be his right hand. At the same time Mack asked again for the bond.

"I was looking for it one day but I didn't find it," answered Benoni.

"You didn't find it?"

"I'll look better. It must have got mislaid.". . .

So Benoni shut up his home and in his spacious leisure took to working at Mack's store.

After all, it was amusing enough to hang about inside that counter, that barrier which he had known from childhood and had never penetrated before now. As the holidays drew near, there were more and more people in the store every day; the farthest counter, where the spirit business was done, was awash from morning to night. Benoni lent a hand where it was wanted, keeping an eye on the experienced assistants, how they went about it, and he was constantly learning something. Even his talk caught a commercial flavour, it was "prime and seconds," "gross and net," all day long.

But the two store clerks who had everything at their fingers' ends looked with considerable annoyance upon this outsider, this Post Benoni, who so often got in their

Benoni

way and so seldom was of any use. They too had *their* cunning and resource: they knew the customers as soon as they entered the door and had a pretty good idea of what each had come for, and they generally managed it so that Benoni had to go to the cellar with the customers who wanted treacle or train-oil or leaf tobacco, while they themselves stayed where they were and dealt with dry goods and cereals and fine things. So it came about that Benoni was away for a good while each time, as the blessed treacle ran so slow in the cold weather.

Rosa had not yet shared in the work; but one busy Saturday morning she came down into the store, stepped behind the counter and stayed there. She had on blue fox furs and wore gloves on her little hands. All the women who came into the store knew her and they thanked her and felt honoured when Rosa parson's daughter inquired about their health. She was not so careful about her sales either and took nothing extra for a rather full length of material or for fourteen dress buttons to the dozen.

"It's welcome to see you here among us," Benoni said to her.

The two assistants were furious. Yes, these sweethearts were going to be a fine help; it would have been far better if the pair of them had stayed away. Now they stood chattering right in front of the coffee drawer which was in and out the whole time.

"It's a very good thing you put on your fur cloak," Benoni was saying to Rosa. "And that you have something on your hands," he said.

Oh, everything was so right that she did, Rosa!

But now there was a man who wanted lamp-oil. That was in the cellar, where all the oil was kept. The two assistants looked at each other and then one of them, Steen, made bold to say to Benoni:

"Perhaps you would be so kind as to serve this man?"

Benoni

"No, no!" said the man, ashamed at the idea. "Hartvigsen shan't go to the cellar himself for my sake. I'd rather go without the oil," he said, humbled to the dust.

But after being shown such respect Benoni had no objection to drawing oil for the man. "I do it for fun," he said; "come on with your can."

The man continued to cry shame on himself all the way for allowing such a thing. "There's no modesty in me," he said; "don't go, Hartvigsen; I'd rather sit in pitch-darkness all Christmas, I would, with me and mine."

However, Benoni was kept a good while in the cellar this time; those wags of clerks loudly asked everybody in the store: "Is there anyone else who wants something from the cellar now Benoni's down there?" One after another was sent down. Benoni began to see through the trick and thought to himself: I'll teach that good Steen to send me on his errands.

When at last he escaped from the cellar smelling of train-oil and tobacco, he had peace for a while and again kept close to Rosa and chatted with her about this and that.

Another man wanted something from the cellar.

"I haven't time just now," said Steen. But then he blundered heavily, only remembering Benoni the postman and writ-server and not the wealthy skipper and master seiner. He said: "But perhaps Benoni will serve this man?"

Benoni looked back at him and answered:

"Wouldn't you like to have a servant to blow your nose for you?"

Steen the clerk turned red as fire and didn't say a word; but Benoni looked from one to the other and laughed exultingly. And he likewise looked at Rosa and laughed; but a pucker showed for an instant above her nose. Then Benoni regretted his coarse mouth and was glad enough if Rosa even listened to the words he addressed to her.

Benoni

Mack looked in from the office, and all the people standing at the counter gave the mighty man a respectful greeting. Benoni wanted to show off before Rosa and the rest, he got Mack a little aside and began of his own accord to talk about the mortgage.

"I can't find it," he said; "I must have lost it."

Mack answered suspiciously:

"You can't have done that."

"I couldn't have left it behind on your desk, could I?"

Mack thought for a moment, suspicious and uncertain:

"No, you put it in your pocket."

"If it's gone astray I must have another receipt," said Benoni.

There was a twinkle in Mack's eye and he replied:

"Well, we can always talk about that."

As Mack turned his back and went out, Benoni said in a fairly loud voice:

"For it's a matter of five thousand dollars net to me."

People were welcome to hear that it was no trifle he was discussing with Mack.

A nice rogue that Benoni! While he stood there pretending concern for the fate of the mortgage, he remembered clearly enough that he had already delivered it to the Sheriff's officer with instructions to have it registered at the first sessions if Benoni himself was away from home.

"That Benoni!" nodded the people at the counter. "Five thousand dollars!"

There he was humping his shoulders and swelling with riches. Why wouldn't Rosa ask him for something? He could buy the whole store for that matter. He asked her again, as he had done more than once, to choose any goods she wanted; Rosa did not avail herself of his offer. He produced of his own accord a piece of specially fine linen; it was of the same quality as his church-going shirts.

"What do you think of this?" he said.

Benoni

She looked at the stuff and at him and at the stuff again. "What I think of this?"

"If you'll have the whole piece you can put it down to me. I don't know, but I believe I have credit enough."

"No, thanks. What should I do with it?"

"Can't you use it for drapery?" he said. And by that he meant underclothing, shifts.

The two clerks looked at each other and had to duck their heads into the drawers. Rosa made no answer; she smiled a little for appearance' sake, but again with that pucker above her nose.

Benoni put the stuff back in its place. There ought to be some limit to propriety, that pucker above the nose was too squeamish altogether. When he had used such a choice word, there could be no question of indelicacy. . . .

But Mack, he had stopped at the window of his office and was still thinking of the bond. He whistled softly and kept one eye open, the other shut, as though taking aim. The good Benoni wished to have the bond registered, but he couldn't find it, he had lost it. Oh, that Benoni, to make sure he ought to take a look in his chest, then he'd find it right enough! And then the paper would go straight to the registry.

Suddenly Mack opens his door and calls in Steen the clerk.

"You will take a half-barrel of cloudberries down to the first south-bound mail-boat," he says. "It's an order. Let the cooper choose the wood carefully. Address it to the district judge at Bodö again, as you did three years ago."

VIII

THEN Christmas Eve came and Benoni was at Mack's party, but Rosa had gone home. She had not said good-bye to Benoni on leaving, but Mack's housekeeper was to be sure and give him messages.

There was no particular Christmas jollity about Mack's capacious drawing-room; Benoni was used to different things. Even if he spent Christmas Eve by himself, he was in the habit of singing a bit of a hymn between drinks and reading the prayers. There was such a dismal expanse of empty space in this room, not even chairs, but only a couple of sofas, as the chairs had been borrowed for the supper table in the dining-room.

According to old custom, Mack had lighted the chandelier with the hundreds of crystal drops and was himself walking about the room in fine clothes and bead-embroidered slippers, quietly smoking a long pipe. He talked, not as yesterday and the day before of the price of fish, of business and bait, but in honour of the occasion of stories and odds and ends he had read in the paper and of his grandfather who had lived for a time in Holland. To go with it, he now and then poured Benoni out a glass of wine and drank one himself.

Then the housekeeper threw open the door of the dining-room; now would they please come in to supper! Mack went first and Benoni followed. He found just as much light here; there was a chandelier in the middle and four pairs of candles ranged down the long table.

The housekeeper opened the door of the kitchen and called out: "Now then, you may all come in!"

Benoni

And in came all the servants and people of the place, quietly and ceremoniously: the farm-hands, the two blacksmiths, the quayside hands, the baker, the cooper, the store clerks, the two millers, upper and under, almost all of them with wives, but without their children; last of all came the two white-haired paupers, Fredrik Mensa and Mons. Of these two ancients, Mons had come first to Sirilund, he was to have stayed his three weeks as a visitant pauper. Oh, yes, it was a long time ago, while Mack was still a married man and his daughter Edvarda was a little girl. But when the three weeks were up, Mons declined to be moved on to other quarters, he appeared before Mack and Madam Mack with bare head and asked to be allowed to stay. "You can stay!" said Mack. Oh, Mack was not one to chase anybody away, that mighty man! So Mons went about the farm and chopped wood and babbled to himself and enjoyed life; well, clothes and food he had in abundance. Mons was a big old man with a stoop, a long-bearded Moses with a hooked nose; he was charitable and gentle as a child. When some twelve years had gone by and Mack's wife was dead and his daughter Edvarda grown up, then Mons was so worn out in arms and back that he couldn't keep all the stoves in wood. So of his own accord he struck up an acquaintance with Fredrik Mensa, who was just as old and worn out, so as to have help with the wood and a little pleasant company in the wood-shed. And then Fredrik Mensa in his turn went to Mack and to Edvarda Mack and stood before them bare-headed and asked if he might stay on. And Mack, he was still the man he had been: "You can stay!" said he. From that day the two paupers lived at Sirilund and kept together and pottered with the wood and fell more and more into their dotage. And if Mons was big and lumpish with his giant's shoulders, Fredrik Mensa was so lean and tall that it was a sight to see, and perhaps that was

Benoni

why his daughter was so pretty and had such a pretty figure and afterwards became parlour-maid at Sirilund. And after that she was married to the under-miller. . . .

It was a crowded supper table. And there were silver spoons and silver forks for everybody, rich and poor alike.

"Why aren't the lighthouse people here?" asked Mack.

"We have asked them."

"Ask them again."

Ellen Parlour-maid, who was an active little body, wriggled instantly out of the door after the Lightkeeper and his wife. Nobody touched the food till they came, there was only a dram drunk, which Steen the store clerk went round and poured out.

The lighthouse couple were a modest, insignificant couple, dressed according to their humble circumstances in shabby, old-fashioned clothes, with faces that the joyless life and pernicious idleness of the lighthouse had rendered imbecile before their time. How tired they were of each other and what hard work it seemed to be civil and keep passing one another the dishes!

Down at the bottom of the table sat the under-miller's wife and she had the two paupers to look after because they were so senile. Ho-ho, twenty years before she had been a regular beauty in the Sirilund household, but now she had put on more fat and had two chins. But she was still nice-looking and she had a fine complexion, there was nothing old about her. Higher up sat Jakobine, who was married to Man Ole. She had come from the South, from Helgeland, she was dark and sharp-eyed and her hair was all in ringlets, for which reason she was called Bramaputra. Nobody would have thought it was the shrivelled lightkeeper who had found this name for her in a happy moment.

Mack sat looking down the table and knew them all. And nearly all the girls and married women he knew right

Benoni

well, and every Christmas Eve he sat there looking down the table at the familiar faces and remembering things.

And don't you think the under-miller's wife had her memories too, as her massive bosom heaved up and down? And wasn't Bramaputra in like manner full of thoughts as she darted fire from her eyes and tossed her curly head? When the brandy came round again, she drank off her glass and grew skittish and reached far out under the table with her toe. But as for Mack, nobody could tell from his steady face that he could ever use his arms in an amiable fashion or be tender in his glances. He raised his glass at proper intervals and he said to Steen the store clerk: "I hope you're not forgetting to fill everybody's glass?" When he saw that the poor cup-bearer had no time to eat his food in peace, he changed his orders and set Martin, the other clerk, to pour out on one side of the table. Mack kept order in everything and his talk was of quiet trifles such as might interest his guests.

Only the two ancients, Fredrik Mensa and Mons, heard nothing, but ate vacantly and stolidly like animals. Mons's head sinks deeper and deeper into his woollen comforter till it looks colossal on his shoulders, Fredrik Mensa's on the other hand towers higher and higher, skinny as a vulture's, but just as devoid of wit as the other's. They are like two dead men come from the grave, their fingers have the sluggish movements of the maggot. When Fredrik Mensa gets his eye on something on the table too far for him to reach, he moves his chair trying to get at it and begins to upset things. "What is it, what do you want?" asks his daughter in a whisper, giving him a nudge; then she puts a piece of food in his hand and that seems to satisfy him. Mons casts a friendly look at a dish of bacon and begins to rake it about; he is instantly helped to a slice. Mons looks at it, sees that for some reason or other it was refractory and hard to

Benoni

catch, but now he has it; he spreads it thickly with butter and starts devouring it. A piece of bread is put in his hand, the maggots fasten upon the bread and keep it. Soon the slice of bacon is consumed, Mons stares all over his plate for it, but it is gone. "You have bread in your hand," says the under-miller's wife, and Mons is quite pleased with this and begins to devour the bread. "Put it in your tea first," they say to him; for everybody is anxious to help the corpses and look after them. Then somebody discovers that it is only dry bread the poor fellow has in his hand and comes to his help with butter and dainties. Mons sits there like a crippled giant, like a mountain, and lets himself be fed; and when he has devoured the slice of bread, he glares at his empty hand and says in the voice of a human: "Is she gone?"—"Is she gone?" repeats Fredrik Mensa like a parrot, as completely imbecile as the other.

These two ancients, their faces smeared with grease, filthy about the hands, smelling of old age, disseminate a loathsomeness beyond measure over their end of the room, a feeling of bestiality which travels along the table on both sides. In any other place but Mack's dining-room all kinds of things might have happened. Not a word of sense is uttered among the guests at that end, all their attention is directed to waiting on decrepitude. Then Mons gets tired of food, he sits staring at the candles on the table and begins to laugh at them. Ha-ha, he says, and his eyes look like a pair of boils. Now I'm dashed if he isn't enjoying himself. Ha-ha, laughs Fredrik Mensa in his turn, prodigiously solemn, and goes on eating. Poor fellows, they can find something to amuse them like the rest of us, say their neighbours. The under-miller's wife is the only one who has enough sense left to be ashamed.

And in the whole big house not a child is allowed to show itself. . . .

Benoni

Then the sweets and the sherry made their appearance. Nothing was lacking at this banquet.

"Are all the glasses filled?" asked Mack. "Then we will empty them, in accordance with custom, to the health of my daughter, Baroness Edvarda."

How correct and genteel and fatherly! Ah, that man Mack, what respect he shed around him!

Benoni sat the whole time keeping an eye on his master, how he coughed into his napkin and not all over the table and how he manipulated his fork. And Benoni for his part was as sharp as a monkey; he fell in with every situation and never went away without having learnt something useful. So when Mack clinked glasses with him, he knew how to return a polished bow and show himself the gentleman. Aye, Benoni was well on the way to becoming Mack's equal.

The host drank with the Lightkeeper and his wife—Sirilund's only neighbours to seaward. Your good health! And the old lady turned bashful and red though she was fifty and the mother of two married daughters with children. The Lightkeeper looked idiotically at Mack with his shrivelled face: oh—I see! He took his glass and drank without hurrying himself. But how strangely his hand shook! Was that because Mack reckoned him as a person one could drink a toast with? Then he sank back into his idiocy.

After that Mack proposed the health of all his people: he would name none and forget none, all had done their work faithfully and he thanked them. A happy Christmas to all!

What a man for a speech! Where in the world did he get the words from? Now the guests were touched, Bramaputra got out her handkerchief. In former years the blacksmith had not cared to drink this toast because he was possessed by an everlasting hatred. Oh, but it

Benoni

was an old story, there were so many mixed up in it, there was his young wife who had come by her death and Mack himself and besides them a stranger whose name was Lieutenant Glahn, a sportsman. It was some years ago now and his wife had been wild about Glahn, but Mack had forced her and did what he liked with her. The blacksmith remembered her still, her name had been Eva and she was a small woman. But he didn't remember much more than that, his daily life had gone on as before, until here he was drinking to a happy Christmas with Mack. And his everlasting hatred had faded out. . . .

"Well, has everyone finished . . . ?" said Mack.

They all got up. Ellen Parlour-maid began at once to carry the white and gold chairs back into the drawing-room, and into the drawing-room went Mack and invited the lighthouse people and Benoni to follow him. All the other guests were invited to spend the evening in the dining-room and drink a glass of two of toddy. Their talk was already lively after the drams and the wine.

"Now if you would play something, Madam Schöning," said Mack, pointing to the little square piano.

No, she could not play. Nothing of the kind. Play? Herr Mack must be joking!

"But you have always played to us before?"

No, no. When? Nothing of the kind. But her daughters could play a little, they had learnt a little after they were married. They were very musical.

"Do you mean to tell me you haven't learnt to play, you, a daughter of a fine family like the Brodtkorbs? Besides, I've heard you myself."

"No, mine isn't a fine family. Fine? How you do joke!"

"Why, your parents owned a whole parish. Do you think I don't know that?"

"My parents? They owned a few farms perhaps.

Benoni

And they had a good stretch of land, but . . . No, Herr Mack, it's only a fairy-tale about that parish. My parents were farmers, we owned a farm at home, we had a few horses and a few cows, but nothing to speak of."

Meanwhile Herr Schöning goes round with spectacles on nose examining the pictures on the walls. He is so cordially indifferent to what his wife may be saying to Mack; oh, how terribly familiar her voice is! They have been married thirty years, they have kept house together for eleven thousand days.

Mack has removed the lid of the instrument.

"No, no," says Madam Schöning. "I haven't played since I was a girl. Unless it was a hymn tune . . ."

She sits down blushing deeply and looking foolish. Mack opens the dining-room door and simply holds up his hand a moment, and all is still.

At the first notes a tiny little jerk goes through the Lightkeeper, he stands still for a moment, staring idiotically at the wall, in defiance, to show he is not going to be disturbed; then he sits down in a chair. But he takes good care to turn his back to his wife. Madam Schöning plays a hymn tune from memory.

When the chorale is finished and played over once more, Madam Schöning collapses and that is the end of her performance.

"Many thanks," says Mack to her. Then he shuts the dining-room door again so that the people in there may be left to themselves.

A huge silver tray comes in with brandy, water and sugar, and Mack says, will the gentlemen please help themselves? He mixes two glasses, one for himself and one for Madam Schöning. Then he goes up to the Lightkeeper and gives him a little of his conversation.

"Yes, that picture there was brought home from Holland by my grandfather."

Benoni

"And over there is a landscape from Malta," says the Lightkeeper, pointing.

"Quite right!" answers Mack encouragingly; "could you see that?"

"Yes."

"How did you see it?"

"It's printed underneath."

"I see," says Mack, realizing that he had underrated the idiot's brains for the moment. "I thought you had been to Malta and recognized it."

Now Madam Schöning in her turn sits cordially ignoring every word her husband utters. Oh, how she knows his skinny back with its prominent shoulder-blades! She begins playing again softly so as not to hear his familiar voice.

"You once commanded a ship, didn't you?" Mack continues, addressing the Lightkeeper. "So I thought possibly you had been to Malta."

A withered smile flits across the Lightkeeper's face:

"Certainly I have been to Malta."

"Really! Fancy that!"

"But if I look at a landscape from Helgeland I don't recognize it merely because I have been in Norway."

"No, he-he, no, of course not!" answers Mack, convinced that this is an idiot to beware of; it is no use making conversation for him.

Mack drinks with Benoni and says a few words:

"You see, my dear Hartvigsen, all these are things that have been handed down, the furniture and that sugar-basin, and the pictures on the walls, the silver and everything about the house. That was the share that fell to Sirilund, the other share went to my brother, Mack of Rosengaard. Oh, well, after my time I suppose it will be sold to the highest bidder. Then you ought to have your eyes about you, Hartvigsen."

Benoni

"That's all according to which of us is going to die first."

To this, Mack only shakes his head. Then he goes over to Madam Schöning again and says she mustn't sit so far off.

But Benoni thinks to himself: now Mack can only have said that to me for the sake of something to say, for he has a daughter to inherit all his means. Then why does he want to give me a fancy for them?

"Yes, you see, Madame Schöning, ever since my poor wife died that instrument has been standing idle. There's nobody here to use it. But I can't throw it out, can I? it's a valuable piano."

Madam Schöning puts a sensible question:

"But didn't your daughter play when she was at home?"

"No, she couldn't. No, Baroness Edvarda had no interests of that sort. And I tell you, I would go such a long way to listen to music! Well, Rosa Barfod plays when she is here; she is musical."

Then Benoni had a great and fantastic idea: what if he went clean against the Baroness and got Mack to do a deal with the piano? He wanted it in his parlour, by next midsummer even he would have a use for it. Had Mack some idea at the back of his head in saying that, he'd like to know? By now the servants in the diningroom were making plenty of noise, playing a game no doubt; both women and men were laughing loudly in spite of the sacredness of the place. A glass was heard to crash on the floor.

"You are interested in pictures," said Mack to the Lightkeeper again. "Now this is on the coast of Scotland. How barren and melancholy it looks!"

"It is very characteristic," said the Lightkeeper.

Benoni

"Do you think so? But it's only rocks and sand, there's no vegetation."

"Oh, yes, there is."

"Here?"

"The sand is finely coloured and there are columns of basalt. But, generally speaking, a good deal grows on rocks and sand."

"A little, I dare say."

"The fir stands on the rocks and draws sap and iron from it day by day. And it does not bend when the storm comes, it simply stands and gives its note to the storm."

"Ah—seen from that point of view," Mack observed, wondering at the other's flow of words.

"There is a plant called asphodelos," continued the Lightkeeper to Mack's further surprise. "Its stalk grows to the height of a man and it has purple flowers. But where it grows, nothing else will grow; it is a sign of dead soil, sand, desert."

"Extraordinary! Have you seen this flower?"

"Oh, yes. I have plucked it."

"Where?"

"In Greece."

"Extraordinary!" said Mack, feeling more and more unsafe with the idiot. "Ah, your health, Madam Schöning!" he said, making a neat escape.

At that moment the tall clock against the wall gave eleven shrill strokes on its little bell.

"Let me mix you another little drop, Madam Schöning," said Mack.

"No, thank you very much, now we must go home to the lamp," answered Madam Schöning; "there is only Einar to look after it."

They talked about this for a while. Madam Schöning

Benoni

had risen and was holding out her hand to say good-bye; but when Mack began asking questions about her son Einar, who was a deaf-mute, she forgot herself and sat down again.

Suddenly the Lightkeeper looked at the clock and said:
"I see it is eleven o'clock; now I must go home to the lamp."

He said this as though his wife had never mentioned the subject, he began at the beginning, made a fresh start; to such an extent were his wife's words empty air to him. He finished his glass, gave Mack his hand and said good night, went to the door and stopped once more to look at a picture. Madam Schöning for her part was in no hurry at all, she said all she had to say to Mack before leaving. Her husband then went slowly after her, simply and solely because at that particular moment he had finished looking at the last of the pictures.

Now Mack and Benoni were alone. The noise in the dining-room was increasing, one of the women shrieked and there was a sound of a heavy fall on the floor.

"They seem to be getting merry in there," said Benoni with a smile. It was as though he himself was totally unconcerned in such merriment.

But Mack made no answer and was not communicative. He closed the piano, breathed on it and wiped it with his cambric pocket-handkerchief. But this he must have done to show what a handsome and costly piano it was.

"Won't you mix yourself another glass?" he said to Benoni.

"No, thank you so much all the same," answered Benoni.

The baker was heard singing loudly in the dining-room. The others tried to make him stop and accused

Benoni

him of being drunk, at which he protested. Only now and then could single voices be distinguished.

"Excuse me a moment," said Mack. "Do mix yourself another glass, I must just . . ."

With that, Mack went out in the direction of the kitchen, probably to give an order. He met his housekeeper, and Benoni heard him say:

"If the baker is feeling tired, Man Ole and the cooper can see him home."

Not a word of reproach, not a sign of annoyance with the unfortunate baker! But that sharp fellow Benoni, he nodded to himself and thought: now Mack gets rid of three of the menfolk at one stroke, and their three wives are left behind!

Mack continued to his housekeeper:

"You'll remember the water for my bath, won't you?"

"Oh, yes."

Then Benoni awoke to the fact that it was getting pretty late and that Mack would soon go up to his room. Yes, Mack's baths were famous, and they were sufficiently frequent for everyone to know about them. He had a soft feather-bed and a pillow in his bath-tub and lay there very comfortably. Oh, there were amazing stories about his bath and about those who helped him and about the four silver angels on his bed.

When Benoni was going to say good night, Mack was still the best of hosts and forced him to have another glass. They talked easily about small matters, and Benoni made bold to ask what a musical box like that piano might cost. But Mack shook his head, he knew nothing about prices of pianos on an evening like this.

"It costs some money, I dare say," he said. "My ancestors never inquired the price so long as they got what they wanted. There's a rosewood work-table in the

Benoni

boudoir, it's inlaid with silver and ebony, you ought to see that some time."

The housekeeper came in again and announced in consternation:

"The silver . . . there are three forks missing this year."

"Yes?" was all Mack said. "Oh, it's the old joke, they like to give us a scare every Christmas Eve. Last year the forks came out right, didn't they?"

"Yes."

"They expect me to find the forks on them myself, they think it such fun to have me search them up in my room and pass sentence on them. It's just an old custom of the house."

The housekeeper was not reassured.

"Jakobine and the under-miller's wife are helping with the washing up," she said. "Then I count the silver and Jakobine starts crying and says it isn't her. And then the under-miller's wife starts crying too for the same thing."

"It's part of the game," replied Mack with a smile. "They're just like children. Isn't the baker's wife crying?"

"No. Well, I don't know."

"Is everything ready up in my room?"

"Yes."

"Then let the baker's wife come first."

The housekeeper departed. Mack turned to Benoni with a smile and remarked, Well, now he'd have something else to think about than sitting over a cosy toddy, he had to go and administer justice. Ah, yes, one must keep up old customs.

Benoni took his leave and Mack accompanied him to the door. Out in the passage they came upon the baker's wife, who was already on her way upstairs.

IX

NEXT morning, before Benoni was up, there was a knock at his bedroom door. He thought it was his old servant who had taken it into her head to show him honour by knocking, and he called out: "Come in!"

In walked a strange man.

"Good morning. Happy Christmas, I should say."

The man made a kind of excuse and pulled off his fur cap. He was a stranger with a little fair beard, thin about the body, long-haired, still a young man.

Benoni lay looking at him and said:

"See and sit you down."

"Thanks," said the man. "It got so cold outside, I was getting frozen. So I thought perhaps I might venture to go and see Hartvigsen."

His speech was ready and straight without being needlessly obsequious.

Benoni asked:

"Do you know me?"

"No. I've only heard about you. Folks said I ought to come to you."

"What's your name?"

"Sven Johan Kjeldsen. I'm from town and I was watchman there for a while, so folks called me just Sven Watchman. But I come from the South really."

"And what brings Sven Watchman to me?"

Benoni was not very sure what a watchman was or how he ranked socially, so to be on the safe side he was rather deferential to begin with.

Benoni

"What brings me is that everybody says I ought to go to Hartvigsen. I'm looking for work and wages. Don't go to Mack straight away, they said, but go to Hartvigsen and he'll speak to Mack for you."

"So you haven't been to Mack?"

"No."

Benoni felt proud and flattered. So that was what folks said: go to Hartvigsen and you'll get a job with Mack!

"I'm not the man that could say the smallest word to Mack for you," he said. "But we'll find some way. How did you come here?"

"On foot, I walked. I have a diamond, here it is, I cut glass. I took a big case of glass with me from town and travelled about putting in windows for folks. But then there wasn't any more glass left."

The man smiled and Benoni smiled.

"That wasn't a job to take on either," said Benoni.

"But you see I had this diamond, I found it in the street one night when I was watchman. And so I wanted to make use of it."

"Well, and then the glass gave out?"

"I used my last bit of glass last night. There was a tiny little house somewhere around here, it had a heart-shaped hole in the door. I put a pane of glass in it."

Benoni began to laugh:

"You put a pane in the . . . ?"

"Just to pass the time. It was such bright moonlight that I had to do something. Yes, I cut a pane and puttied it well in. I wonder if it wasn't at the schoolmaster's."

"Ha-ha-ha," Benoni roared with laughter. Now he was sure the man had made it up.

The man joined in the laugh. Then he shook himself and said:

Benoni

"And then it got so cold outside that I came and knocked at your door. I've been out all night. When I came here last evening it was shut up."

"I was at a party at that Mack's," Benoni explained. "You ought to have been here at midnight when I came home."

"Then I'd gone back to the little house. May I light the fire?"

"Don't you trouble, I'll . . ."

Benoni jumped out of bed, but the stranger, Sven Watchman, cried: "Lie still, lie still!" and began to light up. What an obstinate fellow! Benoni explained that he had a servant for work of that sort, but she hadn't come yet.

"Shall I put the kettle on?" asked Sven Watchman.

"Can you? The servant will be here directly, but . . ."

So Sven Watchman put the kettle on and when it boiled he threw in two handfuls of coffee. "Don't be stingy with it," said Benoni. When the room was warm he got up and brought out food. Then it occurred to him that the stranger must be given the impression that he was in a gentleman's house and Benoni began to wash vigorously. When that was done he produced a bottle of spirits. They ate and drank, both of them, and Benoni thoroughly enjoyed listening to the yarns of this devil of a Sven Watchman. It was a jolly breakfast.

Then the servant came. Benoni poured her out a Christmas dram and said she could thank the stranger for doing the work. "Bring in fresh washing-water," Benoni added.

"For me? I have washed myself," Sven Watchman replied. "I did it in the wood before I came here. I wash myself in snow."

"What did you have to dry yourself with?" asked the servant.

Benoni

"The lining of my sleeves."

"I never!"

"And I did my hair with a dry fir-cone."

"Did you ever hear the like?" said the old girl to Benoni.

This stranger delighted Benoni from the very first. And it did him no harm either that he had come and presented himself in his poverty; so he was no Crœsus who could rattle the silver in his pocket and make Benoni feel small. And the good Sven Watchman was so grateful for everything and had such polite words for every benefit conferred: when Benoni urged him not to be stingy with the coffee Sven replied: Aye, aye, I can see there's plenty of everything in this house. And when Benoni promised to take him to Mack and say a word for him Sven merely remarked—after his best thanks—that that was just what everyone had predicted.

"And if Mack won't take you on, I'll take you on myself," said Benoni.

It was early in the morning and he had drunk two drams, so his heart was big. He went on:

"Maybe I'll be wanting as many men as that Mack, as far as that goes."

But now Benoni could see himself that he was going too far, and he amended:

"There's my big seine hanging there. If the herring comes I shall be thirty hands short."

"Aren't you going to Lofoten?" asked Sven Watchman.

Benoni started. So the stranger had heard that too, that he was to command the schooner and buy three shiploads of fish. His answer was short and to the point:

"If I decide on Lofoten I'll take you with me."

X

BENONI is in Lofoten; all the fishermen have gone to Lofoten, the place is empty of men. Benoni is in command of the schooner and, sure enough, he has taken Sven Watchman with him as one of his hands. And Mack's two sloops have likewise sailed away, one in charge of Villads the wharfinger, the other of Man Ole. There is nothing left in Sirilund bay but a couple of four-oar boats and a big sail-boat that serves as tender to the mail steamer.

Benoni had just barely managed to say good-bye to Rosa; there was so much to be seen to and so many orders to give the last day before sailing that he only had time to say a hurried farewell and that he would be true till death. He turned once more going down the road and called out that he would buy her a ring and a cross without fail. Then he sailed out of the bay and Rosa stood at a window of Sirilund and followed him with her eyes. But after half an hour had passed it may have been only a dress hanging in the window that he saw.

At Mack of Sirilund's there was nothing fresh; but at Arentsen's the parish clerk's it happened one day in February that the son, the legal luminary, came home. Now he had finished his studies. And Young Arentsen had such marvellous white hands and not a hair left on the top of his head, so everybody could see he had been studying hard. And mighty was the respect that surrounded him. He was given an office and a room at the parish clerk's and made ready to conduct cases in a new fashion, polishing them off promptly; henceforward nobody should suffer injustice year after year but should get his rights straight away. Oh, there would be plenty to keep him busy in the country round; the old Sheriff had ridden roughshod over them.

And now the aged parish clerk and his wife would enjoy their ease; and indeed they had toiled and moiled through a long life without giving themselves any rest. Their first six children together had not cost so much as the seventh, the youngest son, Nikolai, the hope of the family, the lawyer. They had slaved and pinched for his sake, gone without food and clothes, spent their last dollars, borrowed on mortgage—now the boy had come to pay it all back. Now his name was put up on the office door and under it the fixed hours when he was to be found.

For the present, Young Arentsen strolled about the roads and looked up a neighbour or two and had a word for those he met to show he was not proud. There was a good deal of fun to be had out of him too, he seemed to be good-natured and easy-going and could tell many a lively story. He put in an appearance at church and made himself known far and wide; but as at this time of year the only grown-up people left about the place were women, he had no callers at the office. For cases he would have to wait till the spring, when the fishermen came home. And until then the place was absolutely without money.

One day Young Arentsen came strolling down to Sirilund. He took his time passing through the yard, stood a long while looking at the doves and whistling tunes to them. As this took place just outside the drawing-room windows, he was observed both by Mack and by Rosa Barfod from indoors. Then he went in. He kept his hat on till he was right inside on account of his baldness.

"Welcome home again, a full-blown lawyer and all,"

Benoni

said Mack to be friendly. And he called him Nikolai like a father.

They talked about one thing and another. And Rosa, who had once passed for his old sweetheart, she was in the room, but he made no more ceremony on that account, his talk was just as light and cheerful as usual. When Mack asked about his plans for the future, he replied that at present the only plan he had was to sit at home and wait for people to lose their tempers. "They owe it to me to start wrangling over something," he said. And Rosa, she knew him, she gave a happy little laugh, though she was hurt that her engagement had not sobered him.

"But it's terrible the way you've lost all your hair," said Mack.

"All?" answered Young Arentsen unperturbed. "Certainly not!"

But Rosa had seen his bald head before, it was nothing new to her. Alas, in all these years she had found him more and more changed with every trip she made to the South. And every time the man had become more of a sham, made up of folly, untrustworthiness, triviality and laziness. The life of the city had turned this peasant lad into a ne'er-do-well.

"Scarce as these hairs may be," said Young Arentsen, passing his hand over his polished crown, "it is not long since they were raised on end. Stood right on end. That was when I came home."

Mack smiled and Rosa smiled.

"The first one I met was Gilbert the Lapp. I knew him at once and asked how he was, how in the world he was getting along. Oh, all right, answered Gilbert; but Rosa, she's engaged to Post Benoni, he answered. To P-o-s-t Benoni? said I. That's so. To me-e-e! said I. But Gilbert only shook his head and didn't agree with me.

Benoni

Well, there you are, judge of my horror when he didn't agree with me."

There was an awkward pause.

"At that moment," continued Young Arentsen, "my hair stood up through the top of my brain-pan."

Rosa went slowly away to the window and looked out.

At this moment Mack had every reason to take down this jaunty upstart a peg or two; but, being a master of reflection, he came at once to the conclusion that after all he did not want to make an enemy of Nikolai Arentsen, the legal luminary. Quite the contrary. But he wouldn't let him run on in this familiar strain either. Mack said:

"Well, I dare say you two have something to say to each other . . ."

With that he left them.

"No, nothing at all!" Rosa cried after him.

"Now look here, Rosa, do turn round," pleaded Young Arentsen. He did not get up and did not even look at her. Instead, he looked about Mack's drawing-room, where he found himself for the first time. "There are some good old engravings here," he said with the air of a connoisseur.

No answer.

"Oh, come on, let's have a little talk," said Young Arentsen, getting up. He went over to one of the pictures on the wall and looked at it closely. The two were standing with their backs to each other. "Upon my word, it's not bad," he said, nodding to himself over the picture. Suddenly he went up to the window and looked into Rosa's face: "Are you crying? Ah, I thought as much."

She left the window and flung herself into a chair. He followed slowly and sat down in another.

"Don't be so sad, little big Rosa," he said; "the whole thing isn't worth it."

Benoni

These tactics were no use. He tried others:

"I sit here talking and talking, but oh, how slow you are to listen to me! You don't exactly trespass on my time. Will you kindly give me the smallest sign that you're aware of my existence?"

Silence.

"No, look here!" he said, getting up. "Here I come back to—my native land in a way, and the first thing I do is to hasten to you . . ."

Rosa looked at him with open mouth.

Young Arentsen exclaimed:

"There I struck a spark out of you! Now you're smiling! Ah me, your glowing copper smile and your warranted lips!"

"Oh, you *are* crazy!" exclaimed Rosa in her turn.

"Yes," he instantly answered with a nod. "Since I came home I have been crazy. Do you know what I have heard about you? That you are engaged to Post Benoni. Have you heard anything to beat it? Crazy, you say. No, paralysed, departed this life straight away. I pass my time sniffing out every reason I can think of, but none of them is any good. As I was coming here to-day, I said a prayer to God. I don't suppose it was much of a prayer and I didn't ask for so very much, but the idea was that I might be allowed to keep my wits. P-o-s-t Benoni! But what about me? Crazy, you say. That's it, crazy and ill. I stand here positively ill in bed. I do. I'm crammed full of illness enough to kill a grindstone."

"But dear me!" exclaimed Rosa, again at her wit's end. "Is there any sense in this?"

He was struck for a moment by the genuineness of her outburst, he winced a little and said in a more subdued tone:

"Well, say the word and with my own hand I'll put my hat on my few hairs and go my way."

Benoni

When she had sat in thought for some moments longer, Rosa held up her head and said:

"Oh, well, it doesn't matter now. But all the same I think your tone . . . You might have been a little more serious. I ought to have written and told you what had happened, but . . . Yes, we are engaged, there had to be an end of it. It doesn't matter."

"Not so sad! Let's have a little talk about it. You know we're the best enemies in the world."

"There's nothing more to talk about. We've talked enough, haven't we? I believe it's fourteen years since we began."

"Yes, when you come to think of it, it's a fabulous fidelity. If you took a flying trip round the human race trying to match such fidelity you wouldn't find it. Well, as I was saying, here I come back to my native land . . ."

"Well, now it's too late. And a good thing too."

Then he turned serious and said:

"So it's the dovecote and the big boat-shed that have decided you."

"Yes," she answered, "one thing and another, I can't deny it. Partly for his own sake too, for that matter. And then there had to be an end of it. And since he wanted me, why . . ."

Pause. Both sat thinking their own thoughts. All at once Rosa turned to look at the clock and said:

"I don't know——"

"*I* do!" he replied, and took his hat.

"You see, Mack may think we're sitting out here getting engaged," she said with great distinctness. Suddenly she was stung by a sort of anger and asked: "Tell me, those wretched examinations, you might have been done with them three or four years ago, they say."

"Yes," he answered shamefacedly; "but then the fidelity would only have been ten or eleven years old."

Benoni

She made a gesture of weariness and got up. He said good-bye without giving her his hand and then asked:

"Not that it makes any difference now, but what if I too went in for acquiring property?"

"Well, why don't you?"

"No, in God's name, this isn't a manifesto. All I say is: henceforth the sum of my ambition shall be a dovecote and a boat-shed."

XI

AT Easter many of the fishermen made a trip home for a week. They brought big Lofoten cod for their wives and children, a single boat might have fish for a score of homes, and besides they brought all sorts of messages from those who had stayed behind. As Benoni could not get away himself, because he had to see about buying three shiploads of fish, he sent home Sven Watchman with a boat's crew and the same Sven was entrusted with the safe-keeping of a gold ring and a gold cross for Rosa Barfod. And Rosa was home again at the parsonage, so the messenger had to walk the whole way through the common to the next parish to get the things delivered. There was a letter with them too.

Sven Watchman stayed at the parsonage over Easter. He brought his good humour with him and sang to the people of the place when they asked him. Fair of beard and fair of skin he was and his limbs were full of strength. He carried water both for the cow-shed and the kitchen.

Once Rosa came into the servants' hall while he was singing.

"Go on," she said.

And Sven Watchman didn't wait to be asked twice, he went on with his watchman's song:

>"How many of our fellows
> Must plough the boundless sea,
> Where tempests toss the billows
> In night's dark mystery!

Benoni

God let them thrive,
The clock's gone five,
And grant them well to wive!"

"Only I must say," he began chatting, "they don't sing round about here. They're just like a lot of animals every day of their lives. When I meet a man and ask him if he can sing, he can't do it. It does make me so vexed sometimes."

"Do you sing all the time, then?" asked one of the maids.

"Yes, I do. I'm not one to hang my head, I laugh and enjoy myself. I'm sure there's plenty worse off than me, let them hang their heads. But I'll tell you one thing: Hartvigsen can sing."

"Can he?" asked Rosa suddenly.

"That he can. When he reads prayers and sings the hymn, there's nobody sings louder than he does."

"Does he sing pretty often in Lofoten?"

"Oh, yes, Hartvigsen sings. Yes, I should say so."

"You must thank him from me for what he sent," said Rosa.

Sven Watchman bowed. Oh, that Sven, he was from town and had learnt manners, so he bows and says:

"Thank you. And there'll be a letter to take back to him perhaps?"

"Oh, no, I don't think so," answers Rosa. "A letter? No, there's nothing to write about here."

"No, no," says Sven Watchman, rather surprised.

No, Rosa didn't know of anything to write about to her fiancé. She had tried on the ring and the size was a good shot but how heavy her hand was with that thick ring on! It made the whole hand feel strange to her. Then she looked at the cross. It was a big gold cross to be worn on a black velvet ribbon, as was the fashion. But then

Benoni

she had a cross already, a little cross that had been given her at confirmation. She wore both the ring and the cross on Easter Day, then put them both aside. The letter she had read once, and after all she hadn't expected it to be different; but she did not read it again.

All the same, perhaps she ought to send Benoni a few words of thanks? That was certainly not too much to ask of her. So in the evening she sat down and wrote nicely and cordially that Dear Benoni, though it is late at night, and so on. And the ring fits and I have put the cross on a black velvet ribbon, and so on. And we are all well at home and now I am so sleepy, good night. Your Rosa.

She would have sent these lines in the morning, but by the time she was up Sven Watchman had already gone. Yes, for Sven Watchman had another letter from Skipper Hartvigsen to Mack of Sirilund and to-morrow was Easter Tuesday, so he had no time to lose.

So Sven Watchman walked back across the common and sang a little and chatted to himself a little and thought about one thing and another and swung his shoulders and walked. He did not make a long journey of it; when he arrived at Sirilund it was still light, though the days were so short. He delivered the letter to Mack and was given orders to stay the night and wait for an answer.

Benoni's letter to Mack was about fish prices, cod's liver, roes and salt, how much cargo he had bought and what the prospects were. Furthermore, he had sold a quantity of the bait herring at a good price. In conclusion Benoni, the coming bridegroom, had inquired about the piano in the great parlour and the rosewood worktable in the little parlour, whether Mack would part with these articles to him and at how cheap a price he might value them. As there were neither instruments nor rosewood work-tables to be got in Lofoten except ordinary

Benoni

deal tables that she could not sew at, Mack would be doing him a favour. Respectfully, Benoni Hartvigsen of the Schooner.

Mack sat down to write an answer, that of course he would miss the piano and work-table in his house; but out of goodwill to Benoni himself and because his dear goddaughter was sighing for the above-mentioned articles, in fact probably could not live without them, he was willing to part with them at a price to be agreed upon later. . . .

In the evening Sven Watchman carried on in the servants' hall and sang songs and made things lively. As soon as he arrived the gay rascal had found a bed for himself up in the loft, on the pretence that he was so mortally tired after his walk. And the dusk began to spread around him and it was nice and warm in the loft, so it may be that Sven Watchman fell asleep. But he hadn't the patience to stay in bed more than a good hour and then he sneaked down again. By now the lights were lit in the room below and at the foot of the stairs he encountered a hot-tempered person. This was the foreman of the farm-hands.

A droll slanging-match ensued between the two.

"I've a good mind to take and throw you out," said the foreman.

Sven Watchman laughed and all he said was:

"Have you?"

"It's my place to keep order with everything in the servants' hall. That's what Mack himself says."

"What have I done?"

"You've been up in the loft, and you're just coming down. . . . Jakobine!" the man called up the stairs.

"Yes," answered Bramaputra from above.

"There, you can hear, she's up there."

"What's that got to do with me?" answered Sven

Benoni

Watchman. "I had to sleep up there after my walk."

"You've no business to. Jakobine is married to Man Ole."

"How should I know that? I'm a stranger here, I'm from town."

"Now I'll tell you something: you're a dirty blackguard who tramps the country."

"I'll have you whipped for your foul mouth," retorted the watchman.

"And I'll have you thrashed," said the foreman in a fury. "Did you get what I said? Thrashed."

"I could have the law of you for calling me a dirty blackguard. In any decent town they'd put you in bilboes," answered the other.

Bramaputra asked from the top of the stairs what they were squabbling about. No sooner had Sven Watchman got an audience to his liking than he grew stiff and strong within; he went up to the foreman and shook his fist quietly under his eyes.

"If you don't take yourself off, I'll dust your ears a little for you," he said.

Bramaputra came right down, unafraid and curly-haired and inquisitive.

"Are you quite crazy, both of you? she asked.

"You shouldn't be so easy in your ways," the foreman warned her. "That Man Ole's only gone to Lofoten, he'll be home one of these days."

Then Sven Watchman looked as if he meant to do something and he asked:

"Did you say anything?"

"No," answered the foreman, "I wouldn't waste words on you, I simply take and throw you out."

Bramaputra interposed, she got her arm under the foreman's and hauled him off.

Benoni

"You ought to be ashamed, both of you," she said. "And it's holy Easter and all. Come along with me."

And the foreman went with her into the servants' hall. Sven Watchman was left by himself in the passage, whistling and thinking things over. In reality it wasn't Bramaputra either, but Ellen Parlour-maid that he had in his head; he had seen her a few times and joked with her and shown her various little endearments. She'll come right enough! he thought, and he joined the others in the servants' hall. Then it was that Sven Watchman began to carry on and sing songs and Ellen Parlour-maid, she came right enough in a little while and stayed through the evening; aye, if it hadn't been for Easter they'd have started to dance without a doubt.

In the middle of the fun Mack himself appeared in the door; he had a letter in his hand. There was dead stillness in the servants' hall and each of them must have wished himself far away, such respect did the old gentleman shed around him. But Mack scarcely threw a glance to one side or the other; he was not a man to show any petty fault-finding with his servants.

"Will you deliver this letter to Hartvigsen?" was all he said to Sven Watchman.

And Sven Watchman, he received the letter and made a polished bow and answered that Oh, yes, it should certainly be delivered.

Then Mack turned and went away again.

The stillness lasted a little while longer, then the fun started and got much worse than before, since they all felt they had had an escape. There Mack had stood, thus he had spoken, exactly like one of us. Oh, that man Mack!

Sven Watchman called:

"Now we'll take the song of O ye Sorosi Lasses. Now join in properly. Remember, after every verse that I sing you're to come in and say, talking, O ye Sorosi lasses! That's the way I learnt it. Now then, I'm going to begin."

"Can't we dance a little too?" asked Bramaputra boldly. That woman had a rare devil inside her.

The foreman of the farm-hands answered ominously: "Aha, that Man Ole's in Lofoten now, but . . ."

"Kiss me to-morrow with your Man Ole," said Bramaputra, wiggling up to him, greedy for a dance.

And the foreman went so far as to look at her and say: "Well, if it hadn't been Easter . . ."

"Kiss me to-morrow with your Easter," answered Bramaputra.

So the foreman took the floor and started to swing her round. And he had some power in a dance, that man. After them came Sven Watchman and Ellen Parlour-maid and after them again two more couples; a boy was sent for who had an accordion and could play, there was a regular dance, aye, they all had great enjoyment of it. But the two white parish paupers, Fredrik Mensa and Mons, they sat in a corner and looked on and were like lifeless bodies from another world. Now and again they talked to each other with question and answer, exactly as if they had something to say. But they were imbecile to a humorous pitch, real champions at it; to them the whole affair looked like a room that had got hold of a lot of people to dance with. Now and then they made a grab in the air with their foetus-like hands to hold the room in its place.

And Sven Watchman—what could have become of him and Ellen Parlour-maid? They had made a bolt, they stood saying nice things to each other and he held her close a couple of times and kissed her. She was so little about the waist and Ellen was her little name; she was a lovely creature. When he spoke fondly to her, her

Benoni

eyes were like eels and she fell in love too. Everything about her was dainty: "You have such cold little hands, it's nice to take hold of them and warm them," he said. "Besides, Ellen is so easy to say, it's a Danish name, Ellen."

How young they were, both of them, and how much in love!

The next day Sven Watchman returned to Lofoten.

XII

YOUNG ARENTSEN is on a long journey. He got up early this morning and now the sun is up he finds himself in the middle of the common, on his way to the neighbouring parish. He goes on foot, it is Saturday and mild winter weather.

How is it—this man learned in the law, what makes him do it? The easy-going Young Arentsen, the idle lounger, why does he give himself all this trouble? God knows. But Young Arentsen says to himself that he is acting in the interest of his business. Hasn't he put in an appearance at his own church to get himself known far and wide, and is he not going to show up at the neighbouring church to-morrow for the same reason? Young Arentsen has plans of administering justice and showing people the law in all the tithings round. True, but isn't it the fact that before spring comes there will be nothing for him to do because all the menfolk are in Lofoten and the district is without money; then what is he worrying about to-day?

Young Arentsen knocks the snow off a tree-stump and makes himself a seat. Then he eats his lunch and washes it down well, and after that he takes two more good long pulls and empties the bottle and flings it away into the snow. Ah, it's a relief to get rid of that heavy bottle! thinks Young Arentsen. And it doesn't sadden him the least that the bottle is empty, for he has a full one left.

Perfect peace in woods and fields on a fair winter's

Benoni

day! By no means dull for once; on the contrary, quite interesting just for once!—Young Arentsen throws his head round and watches, he has heard something. There's somebody coming—hey, what a coincidence! It's Rosa.

They exchange greetings and are both surprised.

"Are you going to us?" he says.

"Yes. And you to us?"

"It is in the interest of my business that I'm going. I must show myself at as many churches as possible to make myself known."

Rosa also finds it necessary to explain:

"I'm going to Sirilund. I haven't been there this year."

But as their first surprise subsided, both felt a great annoyance at having chosen this particular day for their walk. Oh, why couldn't they have had a little more patience! It did not look quite so bad for Rosa, because ever since Edvarda's time, the time when she was still in short skirts, she had been in the habit of visiting Sirilund at short intervals. But Young Arentsen was exasperated with himself and thought: if only I had waited over to-day! Well, but did that mean he wasn't the man to find a way out?

"I had a kind of idea that you might be away from home to-day," he said.

"Oh?"

"And that's why I went. I wanted to hit off your church when you were not there."

Did she see through his fabrication? She laughed and said Thanks, many thanks!

"I guessed you wouldn't care to . . . I wanted to make things pleasant for you for once."

"It's queer how serious you've grown," she said suspiciously. "Do you think it's nice of you to watch your chance of coming to us when I was away?"

Benoni

The old rascal didn't feel altogether at ease in all this seriousness either.

"If you take it in that way I'd rather turn round and go with you," he declared.

They walked a few paces.

"No," she said, "I'd rather turn myself. I have no business to think about."

So they turned again and made for Rosa's home.

They walked and walked, chatting lightly, not falling out about anything. Young Arentsen was feeling cheap after the good pulls he had taken at the bottle.

"You go on. I've got something in my boot," he said, and lagged behind.

Rosa walked a little way, turned round and waited. He came on like a boy, like a dancer, and made a joke about sore feet. Then he went straight for her and asked if she was still engaged to Post Benoni.

Yes, she was. Be quiet, not a word.

"You know quite well it's all bosh," he said.

She looked as if she would give him one back, but all at once she showed such talent for holding her tongue and being well-bred. H'm, she said. And indeed she may have agreed with him.

They went on steadily. Two o'clock came, three, it was blowing a little on the hills, here and there a star began to burst out in the sky. Young Arentsen was chatting quietly and pleasantly again; to tell the truth, he was once more feeling cheap, he had made a bad start in the morning with the bottle, now there was nothing for it but to go on. He was no drunkard; he was only a practised reveller who thought a walk like this required a good supply of liquor. . . . Four o'clock came, the road began to descend the other side of the mountain, it grew milder in the forest, darkness spread over the ground.

Benoni

"I dare say it was bosh," said Rosa suddenly.

He had to think hard, trying to remember what he had said a long time back that she now agreed with. "Oh, yes, all bosh," he answered. "What sort of a husband would he make you? All bosh."

"But *you're* not to say so," she objected hotly. "It sounds downright ugly when you say it."

"Then I won't. . . . It's the mischief with these long walks when you're not accustomed to it; now there's something wrong with my braces. You'll have to wait for me on there."

She walked on. When he caught her up, the moon had risen right in front of them, it was a fine evening.

"There's the moon too," he said with new life in him. And he went on talking nonsense, pointed into space, stopped and said: "Listen to the tempest of stillness!" Soon after, he persisted in his light mood: "Fancy, full moon too! What a fixed stare it has! It must be positively embarrassing for you to be looked in the face by a fellow like that."

"Oh? Why?"

"When you have been engaged to Post Benoni."

She did not answer. Now how could it be that she was so well-bred and did not think of saying anything sharp? Young Arentsen had said: *been* engaged. He said it was all over.

"*Borre ækked!*" came a greeting from the road.

"*Ibmel adde!*" replied Rosa absently.[1]

It was Gilbert the Lapp and he was bound for Sirilund.

"Give them our love," said Young Arentsen.

And Gilbert the Lapp, he did give their love, he went to the first house and to the second house and to the third house and said the same thing: "So it's not going to

[1] Lappish greetings: "Good evening."—"God give it."

come to anything with Benoni and Rosa parson's daughter!" Oh, what a master he was at spreading the news that moonlight evening!

"It was strange that I should meet the Lapp again this evening," said Rosa moodily.

They arrived at the parsonage. Young Arentsen was received as an important guest; there was good food and strong toddy with Pastor Barfod all the evening. And when the toddy had begun to work, Rosa's mother had many a good smile over Young Arentsen and his funny talk.

"Your mother must be very pleased now," Fru Barfod might say.

"I assure you, I never get peace from her attentions."

And Fru Barfod smiled and made excuses for her—poor thing, she is a mother, you know.

"She fits me out with two pairs of mittens."

"Poor thing!"

"Poor thing? Aye, but it's only my tenacity of life that enables me to bear it."

Then Fru Barfod had a real good smile; the legal luminary was such an amusing fellow.

When the parson and his wife had gone to bed, Young Arentsen and Rosa sat up till late. They were now quite of one mind and Young Arentsen had become much more sensible; Rosa had never heard him talk so seriously and connectedly before. It was now taken for granted that after all they were the two to be married; that idea about Benoni was folly. The old habit of fourteen years had brought them together again, and it was very natural. Young Arentsen spoke straight out about their future prospects: they would certainly be good, it would run to a boat-shed and a dovecote too, he-he. The boats' crews that had been home for Easter had taken the news of his return to Lofoten and he had

Benoni

already had letters from men of the district asking for his help. Fancy, they couldn't wait till they came home, for fear their opponents might snap him up, he-he.

Rosa said:

"But what am I to do with Benoni?"

"Ah, what *are* you to do with him!" repeated Young Arentsen, giving another meaning to her words. "That's why you throw him over."

Rosa shook her head:

"It won't do. Well, of course I must put an end to it in one way or another, but . . . I must write to him."

"Not at all. It's not necessary."

"Only a few days ago I had another letter from him," said Rosa. "Wait a moment, I'll fetch it. I haven't answered it, it's going to be so difficult."

Rosa went for the letter. And as she did so, she thought of the ring and the cross and she thought too of the parlour and the big bedroom that Benoni had built on to his house for her sake. Then she thought of a date about midsummer.

"It's rather queerly written," she said apologetically to Young Arentsen as she unfolded the letter. She was serious and quite melancholy. "But it isn't the words or the spelling that matters," she added.

"What does matter, then?"

"The spirit," she answered shortly, to discourage any joking.

But Benoni's letter was so stilted, oh, how difficult it was not to laugh at that curious document! He wrote in this wise, that it was truly with an anxious mind he would grasp the pen in his hand and first and foremost inform her that he was well in health. Next, he had been deeply grieved over her silence with Sven Watchman. And if it had been no more than two lines it would have been a joy to him for the whole winter; but perhaps she had not been in a condition to write. As regards the cargo, he was buying to the best of his ability and stood on Mack's side, but there were many buyers who screwed up the price. . . . "I must tell you that I have procured two pair of doves from the station here to have home with me for our dovecote against the spring. There are two white ones and two blue. From this you can see that you are always and at all hours in my thoughts, nay, that I am true to you till death. Beloved Rosa, if you have a mind to write to me some time then don't forget to put the schooner's name *Funtus* as there are so many schooners and vessels here over the whole sea. Oh, how I would thank and bless you and keep it like a flower in my bosom. For news I can tell you that we have got a good parson, he visits both us who are on board and likewise the fishermen in the most miserable hovels ashore. And we who are tossed on the waves of the sea from morning to night have a life full of responsibility and may expect the call at any time. Thus a Helgeland boat from Remen in Helgeland capsized last Wednesday midday and a man Andreas Helgesen by name was left. The others were saved from the upturned keel though they lost all they possessed and all their gear which was lines. I will now conclude for this time with my simple writing and beg you for a favourable answer as I love you according to all my power and ability. But when you chose me to be your companion for life your eyes were not set upon high degree or learning but upon my poor heart. One more thing I have long thought of keeping from you and not telling you before I came home but now I have considered that it is best I tell you, namely that I have written two letters to Mack and had two answers that we are agreed and that I have thus bought the instrument that you play on and the rosewood work-table in the little parlour. This I shall have

Benoni

carried down to our building to be a poor remembrance of me when I come home. Farewell and write soon. Your B. Hartvigsen, my name. The schooner's name *Funtus*."

"But, good God, why, that's a cave man's letter!" said Young Arentsen, his eyes wide with astonishment.

"I wouldn't say that," replied Rosa. But she felt very awkward and put the letter in her pocket at once.

"For news I can tell you that we have got a good parson," he murmured with a sidelong glance at her.

"Ugh, why did I show it you!" she exclaimed, getting up abruptly.

While she was putting something straight to cover her shame and annoyance, he could not resist teasing her again:

"What was the name of that man, that Helgelander who was left? Andreas Helgesen, I think? Remember that."

Rosa answered from the other end of the room:

"You don't consider all he's done for me. And now he's bought the piano and Madam Mack's work-table for me."

"Yes, now you'll lose them."

"It's not because I shall lose them. But it's because he bought them and put himself to all that expense. No, it's awfully horrid of me, I feel inclined to cry."

"Faugh!" he said in irritation and got up.

Rosa was angered:

"What do you say? Have you no heart at all? Now I'll write to him, I'll go up and write at once. He shall have a little letter, at any rate, for all his kind thoughts of me."

"I'll take the letter to-morrow," replied Young Arentsen.

XIII

IN the morning Young Arentsen again offered to take the letter for Benoni with him, but Rosa declined:

"No, you will only keep it."

"Yes, I shall," he answered. "Did you really write?"

"Did I write? Of course I did."

"Anyhow you mustn't send it. One ought never to give oneself away like that."

"Keep your great discretion to yourself. The letter is to go."

By the time service was over and Young Arentsen had shown himself to the congregation outside, it was too late to start for home that day and he had to accept the clergyman's invitation to stay the night. And that evening Rosa promised to accompany him down to Sirilund.

On Monday morning they started off, furnished with lunch and a pocket flask from the parsonage. Rosa herself had the letter to Benoni with her, indeed she was still determined to put it in the post.

When they reached the houses on the coast, Rosa turned off in the direction of Sirilund, while Young Arentsen continued his way to the parish clerk's. They were agreed upon everything. Before they parted, Rosa had wanted to know when they were to be married. And on his answering that she could fix the date herself, she proposed the 12th of June, when the men would be taking down the fish from drying. On this too they agreed. . . .

Benoni

Then the fishermen came home from Lofoten and shortly after Benoni and the other skippers with their loaded vessels. The fish was sailed straight up to the drying-rocks, where it was washed and the drying began.

Now there had landed from the last mail-boat a queer-looking gentleman, a foreigner in clothes of a large check, with a fishing-rod made to take to pieces and put together again. This was an Englishman, his name was Hugh Trevelyan and his age might be between forty and fifty. He betook himself straight to the drying-rocks and watched the handling of the fish for two days on end, began in the morning and held out till late in the evening. He spoke not a word and was in nobody's way. Arn Drier, who was in charge of the work, came up and gave him the greeting "Peace!" and asked who and what he was; but the Englishman did not appear to see him. He had a boy with him to carry his hand-bag and the boy had been given a bright dollar for his trouble; but now he was almost ready to die, having had nothing to eat all day. So Arn Drier gave him something out of his basket. "What kind of a swell is that?" asked Arn Drier. "I don't know," answered the boy; "he talks like my baby brother when he tells me to do anything, and when I asked if he came from foreign parts he didn't answer. "He'll be one of those play-acting fellows from the fairs," said Arn Drier. . . . The Englishman stood there leaning on the butt of his fishing-rod and smoked a pipe and watched the work; at short intervals he opened his bag and took a drink at a bottle; oh, how he drank and how stiff his eyes were! He drank two bottles a day; now and again he had to sit down on a rock because he was reeling. When two days had gone by and the washing was over, this singular Hugh Trevelyan took the boy with him and departed. He stopped now and then and looked down at the rocks and picked up stones,

Benoni

which he weighed in his hand before throwing them away; around Benoni's home he examined the rocks again very closely and made the boy break off small pieces which he put in his bag. Then he said he was going to the neighbouring parish and the boy showed him the way through the common and over the mountain; the boy got two dollars for it. Now the Englishman put together his fishing-rod and began to fish for salmon in the big river. There was a wheel on the rod and he wound the fish up out of the water. When he had caught his supper he went up to the nearest farm-house and asked if he might have the use of the fire-place. He cooked the salmon himself and ate it; afterwards he brought silver coins in his hand and paid. And the owner of the farm was Marelius of Torpelvik; he made a contract with the foreigner for free fishing all the summer. Marelius got many bright dollars for this, the Englishman was not close about money. For that matter there was both *Hon.* and *Sir* on the letters that came for this Englishman in the course of the summer, so he can't have been any common person. He settled down in a little cottage on the farm, after paying the occupants to move out. He was sober for two months, then he sent to Sirilund for spirits and drank hard for two weeks, after which he kept sober right on to autumn. He was a man of few words.

That was the only unusual thing that happened in the district. Mack's fish got drier and drier, and the drying-money, the blessed daily wage for wives and children, dribbled safely into the fishermen's homes and was a great boon. This was what happened every year. . . .

And Rosa, she was now at Sirilund and now home at the parsonage, and often she went for walks along the road with her fiancé Young Arentsen. The letter to Benoni had not been sent. No; once, sure enough, it had

Benoni

been her fixed determination to be honest and put the letter in the post, but her inner warmth cooled off and day after day the letter lay there, till at last she put it away. And no doubt Nikolai was right, one ought not to give oneself away like that. She ended by feeling less guilty: Benoni would have to bear his lot as she had had to bear hers for fourteen years; such was life. But time after time she had wanted to confide in her godfather Mack, only he wouldn't listen. These are matters I don't understand, he would say with a wave of the hand. But Godfather Mack had understood well enough when he got her engaged to Benoni? Ho-ho, Mack had a pretty good idea of what was happening! Why, the whole countryside knew all about it, a few cautious words dropped by Gilbert the Lapp had swollen into a broad river of gossip. Nor was Rosa annoyed that people knew the story, it saved her any explanation, it relieved her, she got over it more comfortably.

But Rosa did not always feel safe on her visits to Sirilund, sooner or later the day of reckoning might come.

Benoni had been immensely active from the very first day he came home and had had the piano and the worktable carted home; the only condition Mack made was that it should be done late in the evening. For that matter Mack had been obliging and reasonable about the price, three hundred dollars in all for these heirlooms, these treasures which were well-nigh priceless.

When Benoni was nevertheless a little staggered by the price and declared that he hadn't so much ready money, Mack merely gave a toss of the head and answered:

"My dear Hartvigsen, we have a running account, you know. . . . By the way, there's another thing; have you bought silver, have you thought about that?"

"I've bought her the ring and cross," replied Benoni, and he began twirling his own new ring on his right hand.

Benoni

"But not the silver? What do you expect her to eat with?" asked Mack.

Benoni thrust his hand into his shock of hair and couldn't find an answer.

Mack went on:

"I don't mean to say that what you have may not do very well, and no doubt Rosa would be quite ready to use a horn spoon if it came to that. But the question is whether you, Hartvigsen, are so utterly impoverished that you can offer her a horn spoon and an iron fork."

"To be sure, I never thought of that," mumbled Benoni shamefacedly.

Mack said curtly and decisively:

"I'll let you have some silver."

Then he took his quill pen and began to make a calculation.

Benoni thanked him, he had helped him, had saved him from an awkward predicament. And it might be a great satisfaction to know that he owned the silver that was used at his wedding.... "But not too much," he said to Mack; not a scrap more silver than what I can answer for, if that's what you're reckoning up."

"I'm reckoning what is the least an impoverished pauper like you can stand," replied Mack with flattery. "And I really think you ought to be a little ashamed of yourself. Well—for the sum of a hundred dollars you can have what is indispensable."

"Then that makes it four?" said Benoni. "I haven't got it."

Mack began to write a document.

"You mustn't write that four hundred's to come off the five thousand!" cried Benoni. "You must write it separate. I shall pay you the first thing."

"Good." ...

Benoni was now the possessor of many precious things

Benoni

and it was a wonderful joy to him to walk about his room and look at them. And one of the spoons and one of the forks which struck him as specially handsome were to be Rosa's for every day and not to be mixed with the others. He tried how they would suit her mouth, and wrapped them up separately. Oh, Rosa should have a proper surprise! But the days went by and Rosa did not come; he wrote to her and still she did not come. Then he began to cogitate about it. And now he could not help hearing what was said on every hand about Rosa and Young Arentsen. He treated it as impossible, an empty rumour, a dirty lie, in fact; but there was great uneasiness in his heart. Hadn't he got the whole thing ready for her, the house, the instrument, the silver forks and spoons, everything? Even the doves were on the spot, they walked about the yard and climbed up and flapped back to their house in heavy flight. What amusing beasts they were, these real doves! They swayed in their walk like regular dancers in the ring, and when all the birds sat in a row on the roof of the boat-shed, it was the least of their tricks to make a mess of a whole wall in their innocence.

But the days went by. . . .

One afternoon Benoni was dodging backwards and forwards on the road to the parish clerk's. Then he met Rosa.

Yes, Benoni was out for a walk. Spring was coming on, all the ice was gone, the fiord shone bright and blue, the birds of passage had come and the magpies hopped across the fields with wagtails' antics and chatted and laughed all day long. So spring had come. And Benoni had heard much gossip about Rosa, his sweetheart, and for a whole week he had held himself in until to-day he went out for a walk.

They met and their faces turned pale, both his and

hers. She noticed at once the heavy ring on his right hand.

"So you are out for a walk," said Benoni after he had greeted her and taken her hand.

"Yes. How fit and well you look after your trip to Lofoten!" she said for her part, to soften him a little. Her voice was unsteady.

"Do you think so?"

And now Benoni thought he would behave as if nothing had happened, he wouldn't believe all the gossip he had heard; wasn't this Rosa, his sweetheart, standing beside him? He put his arm around her and tried to kiss her.

"No——" she said, and turned away.

He did not try again, but let go of her and asked:

"Why not?"

"No——" she answered.

Then he got angry and said:

"I'm not going to beg for your sweetstuff."

Pause.

She stood with her head bent and he looked at her the whole time and worked himself up.

"I was expecting to get a few words from you in Lofoten," he said.

"Yes," she replied with a faint heart.

"And since I came home you've been nowhere to be seen."

"I'm not surprised at you," was all she said.

"What am I to believe or think? Is it all over between us?"

"I'm afraid so."

"I have heard a little about it," he said with a nod; he didn't take on any worse than that. "You don't remember your promise?"

Benoni

"Yes, I do remember, but . . ."

"And you don't remember that I put a mark in the almanac?"

"Did you? What mark? Oh . . ." she said, beginning to understand.

"I marked the day you said yourself."

She shook her head slowly: yes, it was dreadful.

"The day we should have been wedded," he said, and tortured her a little more.

Then she moved a pace or two along the road and began:

"What am I to answer! I suppose we don't suit each other, I don't know. Of course it's not the right thing to do what I've done; but there's no help for it. Think of how it would have turned out. For God's sake, Benoni, you must forget all about it."

"Aye, you can find plenty to say now," he said; "I'm afraid I can't chop words with you. But folks say it's that Nikolai Arentsen that's to have you?"

To this she made no answer.

"And he's well used to you, they say."

"Yes, we've known one another a long time. Since we were children," she replied.

Benoni looked at her oval face with its big glowing lips; her bosom went out and in, she kept her eyes dropped so deeply that the lashes appeared like a little line across her face. Oh, iniquity must have taken a great hold on her since she had a mouth like that.

His lips trembled from sheer emotion so that the yellow walrus teeth glistened behind them.

"All right, that Nikolai took you first, so he can have you last," he said to show his indifference.

"Yes," she said quietly and felt relieved. Now it was done; there was nothing more to be said.

Benoni

"He didn't exactly have to go on his knees to get what he wanted, that Nikolai," Benoni went on excitedly. She looked up questioningly.

"That's what folks say. So I don't estimate all your ladylike airs more than a bit of dove's dirt. You'd better go back and give him some more."

She stared at him, her face grew big and innocent; this lasted a moment and then came a sudden change and her eyes flashed.

Benoni saw what he had done and was a little disconcerted.

"That's what folks say," he said. "I don't know. It won't be my affair."

"You're crazy!" she exclaimed.

He regretted his words, and his tongue began to wag again, he babbled on and made himself ludicrous in his confusion.

"Damned if I thought you'd take it to heart like that!" said he. "Do you think I'm such a swine? But, you see, it's practically impossible for me to stand here and talk to you in a goody-goody tone, I must tell you. You don't give a thought to my poor heart, you only listen to the gossip I let out. But it isn't anything to worry about," he consoled her.

She calmed down. As she stood there, a couple of tears trickled down her nose and fell on her bodice. Suddenly she held out her hand without looking up and said simply Good-bye. Then she hurried on a few paces.

"You mustn't believe that," she said, turning.

"What mustn't I believe? No, I don't believe it, and never have believed it. But now you're only thinking about what concerns yourself; you don't pay much attention to all I've got to go through in the course of my long life. I'm not a person worth talking about any more."

Benoni

"I have behaved very badly to you, I know."

"Yes, you know it and know it, but you don't want to talk about it. You're too proud for that with a poor man like me. And now you're going to leave me here. Well, I think it's pretty off-handed of you; but I don't suppose you think so."

When he received no answer to this, his vexation and his bounce swelled up in him and he said:

"Well, well, that Benoni and I'll have to get over it!"

She walked on a step or two, turned and said:

"And I'll send you back those things, you know."

"What's that?"

"The ring and the cross."

"You needn't trouble. No, you've been given them and so they're yours. And as concerns me, why, with God's help I'm not so hard up as that."

She only shook her head and left him.

XIV

BENONI stood there for a while, uncertain what to do. His first thought was to follow Rosa; but the devil might do that, not he! Then he decided to go to the parish clerk's, though he had nothing to take him there. No, it was certain that Benoni was no longer as straight in the back as a monument and he could not go on boasting in his playful way that he had unfortunately won the heart of Rosa parson's daughter and couldn't get rid of her any more.

When he came in sight of the parish clerk's house, he stood and looked at it for a few moments, idiotically, with his head thrust forward; then he came to himself again, turned round and went back to Sirilund to find Mack.

"I just happened to be out to see after something," said Benoni.

Mack thought for an instant and must have seen it all. But he was not Mack for nothing; he laid his quill pen on his desk and asked:

"It's your wages, isn't it? We haven't settled up yet. Would you like to take it in cash?"

"Well, I don't know. There's one or two things; I've come up against such a lot that I hardly know if I'm standing on my head or my heels."

"There's no reason why you shouldn't have your wages," said Mack, taking up his pen again to make a calculation.

Benoni must have been full of thoughts; the next

Benoni

thing he said was: "In Lofoten they were talking about a bank or something of that."

"A bank?"

"Yes. That it was safer. That was what they were saying."

Then Mack stood up suddenly and let a smile play over his mouth as he asked:

"Safer?"

"For the reason that the bank puts the money in an iron chest which can never get burnt up," said Benoni, getting well out of it.

Mack opened his desk and took out his little cash-box.

"Now that's my safe," he said. "And it was my father's and grandfather's before me," he added. Finally he took the cash-box and put it back rather noisily into the desk with the words: "And it has never been burnt."

"No, no," said Benoni; "but suppose accidents were to happen?"

"Then you have the bond!"—But here Mack suddenly remembered that of course the bond was lost. And to avoid raising the question of its turning up and of the registry, he hurried on: "For that matter, I don't keep a lot of wealth in a cash-box. I put out my money, use it."

But Benoni was far too preoccupied for argument; he began all at once to talk about the instrument, the silver and the rosewood work-table; perhaps he would have no use for them, perhaps they would be standing there for nothing. There was this about Rosa and Young Arentsen . . .

"What about Rosa?"

"Folks say so many things. That Nikolai the parish clerk's son has come home and he's to have her, they say."

Benoni

"I haven't heard that," said Mack. "Have you spoken to her?"

"Yes. Precious unobliging she was."

"These women!" said Mack thoughtfully.

Benoni thought in round figures of all he had done and all he was going to do for Rosa, he spoke as an injured party, an offended man, his excitement gave him back his natural speech and he said what had to be said:

"Is it lawful to behave like that to a man of the people? If I took my rights I'd give that Nikolai as much law as his back could carry."

"Has Rosa said anything definite?"

"No, not a word definite. She talked me round with talk. No, she didn't say in so many words that it was to be all over, but that's what she was driving at."

Mack went to the window and thought.

"There's an old saying that women's wiles have no end. It seems to me that women's wiles have a middle and ends too."

It did not suit Mack to exchange chat and confidences with any Benoni on earth. He turned from the window and said curtly:

"I shall speak to Rosa."

A little hope fluttered in Benoni's heart:

"Yes, yes, thank you for that."

Mack nodded that there was nothing more and took up his pen.

"But then there was that about the instrument and the other. Because it's not going to be any use to me if . . ."

"Just let me speak to Rosa," said Mack.

"Yes, yes. And then the bank . . ."

"Stands over."

Benoni went to the door, turned his hat round a couple of times and said reluctantly:

Benoni

"Well, well. . . . Peace be with you!"

Benoni went home; there was not much manly courage in him, he had never felt so low. Next day he called again at Mack's to hear some news; Mack had not had a chance of speaking to his goddaughter. That was funny, thought Benoni; but perhaps Mack meant to work upon her slowly, day by day. Benoni waited two days and went to Mack in tense excitement. He knew now that Rosa was no longer at Sirilund, he had seen her himself on her way to the common.

Mack received him with a shake of the head:

"I can't understand the girl."

"You've spoken to her?"

"Many times. I venture to say that I have put your case strongly. But . . ."

"Well, well," said Benoni, crushed, "then that's the end of it."

Mack was thinking at the window. Meanwhile Benoni began to flare up; he grew proud and angry:

"She was going to send back the gold ring and the gold cross, she told me. You needn't trouble, said I, I've given it you and you can keep it. I dare say I'll have enough for food and clothes all the same, said I, ha-ha. I dare say I'll have a drop to wet my porridge all the same, said I."

Benoni gave a little laugh of exasperation.

"Ah, but I haven't played my last and strongest card," said Mack, turning round. "It will soften her, you'll see," he said, giving Benoni hope.

"You don't say that?"

Mack nodded with compressed lips.

"Asking your pardon, what kind of a card might that be?"

But then Mack waved him off. No chat. He said:

Benoni

"Leave it to me. . . . As regards that bank you've been talking about, is it your intention to call in the money you have lodged with me?"

"Well, I don't know. I'm feeling so low-spirited about the head."

"I want to know one way or the other. Here I am, working for your interests, and I must have leisure to think about them, so I want to have this matter settled."

"No offence meant, I'll let the money be, I don't need it yet awhile."

Benoni guessed that he'd better not go any further just at present, he'd have to wait till Mack had finished his parleys with Rosa.

There was still hope. Mack was so uncommonly almighty.

As Benoni left the office he noticed that Steen the store clerk was putting up a bill on the wall of the store.

"What's the news?" he asked.

Steen only muttered and made no answer.

Benoni saw that it was a sessions notice and stopped to read the date. He felt that that wretched Steen had a grudge against him since that time last winter when they stood together behind the counter, so he didn't care to ask him any more. But Steen was in no hurry about the job, he put his big blue hand over the bill and knocked in each tack elaborately through a little square of leather, there was no end to it. Had it been in the old days, the days of his greatness, Benoni would have thought nothing of pushing the skinny Steen aside with his hand; but now he was sorely stricken and humbled in his heart and he hadn't the pluck to quarrel with anybody. He had to leave the spot without having seen the date.

Aye, verily God had cast him down into the depths. There he was with his great means and his costly treasures, but there was none to share them with him. There

Benoni

was no doubt Rosa wanted to be quit of him; if only he had never raised his thoughts so high as winning her! And how could it turn out well, when at the very beginning he had lied about her being his, at Holla, when he was carrying the Royal Mail? Oh, those blissful days with the Royal Mail, the bag with the lion, when he brought people their letters and was friends with everybody! In winter the common lay still and white and full of snow under the northern lights; in summer it smelt of bird-cherry and pines, refreshing to the soul. It was like a meal of strong sea-birds' eggs.

XV

BENONI went through some bitter days, he grew lean and pale, his brutal health was shaken. He peeped into the many drawers of the rosewood work-table and said: "What am I to do with this?" He rubbed the silver and rubbed the piano and said in the same shattered way: "What good does this do me?" He tried to play it himself, he made his servant come and touch the keys gingerly; but no music came of it and he said: "Hush, somebody might come and hear us!"

At night too he lay thinking of a thousand things: what about it, he thought, I can take another girl! He went over all the marriageable girls round about and was sure he could count himself good enough for any one of them. They were not likely to say No to Benoni Hartvigsen, ha-ha; they knew pretty well that with him there'd be a drop to wet their porridge and some decent drapery goods too, ha-ha. He'd seen how it was every time he'd been out to Christmas dances or at church, his amorous advances had never been declined. But then—there were his big rooms, and there was the instrument, and there was the work-table and the case of silver forks and spoons. And above all—how everybody would crow over his fall if he descended to a girl of humble condition! And Rosa too, she would nod and say: now he's got what suits him! She shouldn't have that comfort. . . .

In his great distress Benoni would have to take to religion or drink. It was a choice between life and

Benoni

death. Oh, but he had such a poor talent for vice, he was a middling sort of man and a good soul. Then again he might go to sea. And that might be the very way to serve her, Rosa, that infamous young lady with no heart. . . . With gloomy looks he said to his servant:

"You're not to leave out any supper for me this evening."

"So you're going to a party at Sirilund again?"

"No. H'm. But I shan't be hungry."

"Well, I never!" his servant exclaimed in surprise.

"I can't be hungry at all hours of the day," said Benoni with irritation. "It's not possible."

"Well, well."

Then he said: "We've all got to die some day."

"Die?"

"Yes, you too. But you don't think about it."

The old girl confessed that, sad to say, she didn't think enough about death, but she hoped one day to be made white as snow in the rosy blood of the Lamb——

"Well, now you're speaking in a general way," answers Benoni. "But I was thinking of shipwrecks and meeting your death at sea."

Oh, yes, she knew about that too, she had a brother-in-law——

"So you're not to leave out any supper," Benoni cut her short.

He turned his steps to Sirilund. What did he want there? The sea lay just outside his front door, if that was what he was looking for. He cast a glance around, at the quays, Sirilund farm, the drying-grounds where the vessels lay, and knew that he had a share in all this wealth, that he was part-owner with Mack. He went up to the farm and asked for Sven Watchman.

Sven was still at Sirilund. When he came back from Lofoten with the *Funtus* and had been paid his wages, he was unable to leave the place for the reason that Ellen Parlour-maid had become so dear to him. He might have taken the mail-boat to the South there and then sailed away from her; but instead of that he went back into Mack's office and stood before Mack himself with a request that he might stay. "What can I use you for?" said Mack, and thought. "For what you please of every kind of humble work," answered Sven Watchman with a polished bow. "There are all sorts of things to be done on your great estate," he went on; "the garden wants finishing, there's this and that to be painted, perhaps a pane of glass to be put in now and then." Mack liked the young fellow, he was a bright and civil creature, so he stood and thought it over. "And then there's the two old men," continued Sven Watchman; "they're nearly dead, they can't manage the firewood. Mons has taken to his bed for good; he's been in bed three weeks and done nothing but eat, they tell me, he'll never get up again. And Fredrik Mensa sits by his side all the time and curses him for not getting up. But he doesn't do anything with the wood either. The other day Ellen Parlour-maid had to go out to the wood-shed herself. But, my goodness, how much can her innocent hands get through!" "Then what are the farm-hands doing?" Mack asked. "They're carting manure; there's every kind of thing to be done on your great estate." Then Mack said: "You can stay."

So Sven Watchman went about the farm and did odd jobs. The maids often wanted a helping hand in the storehouse or the dairy, and how easily it might happen that when Ellen Parlour-maid was doing the rooms a curtain would come off the hooks or a door-handle want oiling! Then she went in all innocence to find Sven Watchman and get his help. And she was truly in love with her merry boy, by all appearance.

Benoni

So one would have thought that the farm-hands and Man Ole and Martin the store clerk would be thankful to have this handy man about the place; but far from it, they persecuted him with their jealousy and did him all the mischief they could. When Bramaputra was washing clothes in the wash-house and asked Sven Watchman to carry the tubs up to the drying-loft, Man Ole crept after him and cried out in his mean way: "Devil take you, how dare you squeeze my wife!" And in the same way the foreman kept a sharp eye on Ellen Parlour-maid and saw that she had never broken so many blinds until she had this Sven Watchman at her beck and call to mend them again. Oh, but Mack himself should hear of it one of these days. . . .

Benoni was looking for Sven Watchman for the sake of hearing a cheerful and pleasant word in his abandonment. He said:

"You're not to mind me, I'm only loafing about these days. I don't want you for anything."

"Loafing about is just what a man like you can afford to do," answered Sven Watchman. "And thanks for the trip with the *Funtus*."

"Ah, the *Funtus*. . . . Now you see this ring of mine. I haven't the heart to take it off again."

Sven Watchman looked up and understood it all. Then he set himself to console his skipper as well as he could.

"No, don't take it off," he said. "There's so many people who come to regret that they acted too rashly and didn't wait awhile."

"Do you mean that? Maybe you're right. I haven't the heart either to cross out a mark I made in the almanac. What do you think about that?"

"You ought never to do the like of that!" said Sven Watchman promptly. "What you put there stays there."

Benoni

"Do you mean that? But womenfolk and all that, they're so different."

"Just so. I don't know what it is about them, they're not steady. It's like when you relieve your feelings and find yourself left with an empty pair of hands."

"No, you're wrong there, it's not so," answers Benoni. "As far as Rosa goes, she's steady, I can't say she isn't."

Sven Watchman was beginning to see how hard was his skipper's case: Rosa had thrown him over sure enough, but she was faultless all the same, Rosa was constant, Rosa was true.

"You'll see it'll turn out all right," he said. "As far as that goes, I'm in a doleful mood myself these days. I should never talk about it if it was in town; there were plenty of girls there, three or four at least. But here there's only one."

"Is it Ellen Parlour-maid?"

Sven Watchman nodded that it was she. And he confessed at once that he had not had the strength to take the mail-boat and sail away from her.

"Then all you've got to do is to stop," said Benoni in his turn. "And then you'll get her all right."

To this Sven Watchman replied that there was both a yes and a no to it. If he didn't get her himself, he wouldn't have her. He had a suspicion that Mack himself was after her.

Benoni shook his head: that was the regular thing at Sirilund. That was not a thing to talk about.

Pale and with trembling lips, Sven Watchman gave an account of his suspicions. It was one morning when he was working in the garden; Ellen Parlour-maid was doing something upstairs, in the passage, and she was singing and humming off and on. Then Mack rang the bell in his room. . . . "I was down there in the garden

Benoni

working and I thought to myself, why should she be singing? It was just the same as saying, Here I am! I hear Ellen go into Mack's room and stay there several hours."

"Several hours? No, that's not likely."

Sven Watchman pulled himself up. He began himself to think it was unlikely and made an effort to be more accurate. "Well, half an hour or a quarter it was at least," he said. "It doesn't make much difference. But when she came out she was heavy and slack about the eyes. I called to her and asked: What were you doing in there? I was rubbing his back with a wet towel, she said, and she was short of breath. You didn't want several hours for that, I said. Or perhaps it was half an hour I said, but that doesn't matter now. She wouldn't answer any more, only stood there looking slack."

Benoni considered a moment and said:

"Now I'll tell you something, Sven Watchman: you're a bigger fool than I thought. Why, she'd worked herself tired over his back and that's why she was slack, poor Ellen."

Benoni spoke severely, so wishful was he to bring consolation to Sven Watchman.

"Do you really think so, Hartvigsen? I thought about that myself, but . . . Perhaps you haven't seen Mack's bed that he catches them in? I was in his room one day to oil the lock of the door. There stands the bed, you see. It's got red silk curtains and a silver angel on each of the bedposts."

Benoni had heard about the four big silver angels; they were old and had been bought in foreign parts long ago. Formerly, in Madam Mack's time, these angels had stood in the big parlour, each on its pedestal, holding candlesticks with candles in their hands; now Mack had set them up on his bed, like the libertine he was.

"Did you ever hear the like?" said Benoni of the angels.

"And the bell-rope's just over the bed," Sven Watchman went on. "It's made of twisted silk and silver thread and the handle's covered with red velvet."

"I never!"

Benoni turned thoughtful all at once: perhaps he could get a bell-rope like that if Rosa . . . But then Rosa was . . .

"How I do talk!" exclaimed Sven Watchman, who noticed the other's melancholy. Besides, he was himself considerably relieved since his skipper had found little Ellen innocent. . . . "I haven't told you the joke about the schoolmaster," he said. "You know I put in a little pane of glass for him on Christmas Eve, ha-ha."

"Has he been here?"

"Aye, that he has. Mad as you like. I offered to sing to him; no. Offered to take the pane out again; no."

"What did he want, then?"

"He wanted to summons me. Hartvigsen, you're a great power here; what shall I do?"

Benoni brightened up at these words and answered in a fatherly way:

"I'll have a word or two with the schoolmaster."

"He said he'd go straight to the new attorney, Arentsen, and have the law of me at the Sessions."

"To Arentsen? That Nikolai of the parish clerk's? When's the Sessions?" . . . Benoni thought a moment, then he said with a formidable look: "He'd better not try."

He went round to the store and read the notice; the Sessions would be held at Sirilund on the 17th. There

Benoni

was only a bare couple of days left. As he stood reading, Gilbert the Lapp came up beside him. He had already been at the spirit counter in the store and was very smiling and pleased with himself.

"*Boris, boris!*"[1] he said in greeting. "And I can give you news of Rosa parson's daughter."

Benoni stared at him.

"The latest news too; I was talking to her yesterday evening," continued Gilbert slyly. "Yes, it's big news. Ho-ho! Have you heard it?"

Benoni's only answer was an uncertain No.

"She's to marry the Attorney," said Gilbert with a laugh.

"I know that," said Benoni.

"When they're taking down the fish from drying, I shall have my wedding, says she."

"Did she say that?"

"I stood as close to her as I'm standing to you. What do you think of that, Gilbert? said she; on the 12th of June I'm to be married, said she. And she laughed and was quite pleased, so she's all right."

Benoni left the Lapp and went home. He thought in his bewildered brain: it's two days to the Sessions, then the mortgage deed will be read out; what will Mack say to that? Then he won't take my part with Rosa any longer. What then? Pleasant journey to her, Rosa was lost anyhow, she was to be married on the 12th of June when they were taking down the fish from drying. He'd have to get used to that idea, and a pleasant journey to her once more! Was he to be just like an ass in the Bible for folks to ride on?

He came home, flustered and exasperated worse than ever. His servant had gone, there was no food left out. He found something to eat and went to bed.

[1] Lappish: "Good luck."

Benoni

Next morning Benoni went out; he would go and see the Sheriff's officer after all and get his mortgage back. No, it was no longer good-bye and pleasant journey to Rosa and all, it would not do to irritate Mack by publishing the document.

But the Sheriff's officer had sent the deed away at once, it had long ago reached the hands of the District Judge. This was a blow to Benoni. "It must be a kind of fate," said the Sheriff's officer, "that you should be balked like this. You can understand that I couldn't keep such a valuable document any time; what if it had burnt up?" Benoni asked him to try to get it back at the Sessions before it was read out. "I don't want it published," said Benoni; "try and get it back, I'll make it worth your while."

Then Benoni went off to the schoolmaster's. Oh, he'd soon bring the worthy schoolmaster to reason. He hadn't said anything about it to Sven Watchman, but he knew in his own mind that the schoolmaster had borrowed money of him, a few dollars last spring, and that would make things easier. No, he hadn't said anything to Sven, he had only promised his help with a look of might. That was the way Mack of Sirilund would have acted, making his power seem a great and mysterious thing.

And naturally, at a word from Benoni, the schoolmaster promised to withdraw the case from Attorney Arentsen. It was just a piece of hastiness, nothing more; he had been annoyed with this vagabond who had made his wife and children believe in ghosts on Christmas Eve, and himself too, half and half.

Finally Benoni hired a boat and was rowed out to sea, to the outlying stations, to inquire about herring.

XVI

IT was not only the schoolmaster and Aron of the Hope[1] who came to Attorney Arentsen with their trumpery cases, the whole country-side was doing it. It became the fashion to take all one's grudges to the parish clerk's house, and Nikolai sat and wrote and did sums for them and drew up papers and took his fees with a liberal hand. Never had squabbles and summonses flourished to such an extent: the loan of a boat without asking leave—as in Aron of the Hope's case—an encroachment on moorland pasture, a trifling error in an account were the sure and instant prey of the pettifogger. It was such an uncommonly fine opportunity; hadn't Nikolai the parish clerk's son finished his long apprenticeship and come home again for the very purpose of getting people their rights, so how could they be content to go along in the old way? With the Lofoten wages and the drying of Mack's fish there was money coming in, ready money big and small, which enabled even the poor man to go to law a little and have a "case" against somebody; why, even Man Ole at Sirilund with his pockets full of wages had applied to Attorney Arentsen to have the law of his wife and Sven Watchman.

And Attorney Arentsen kept his regular office hours and received them one after the other like one in authority. He was no longer easy-going and jocular, but curt and decided. I am Nikolai Arentsen, the Law, he

[1] Hope (Norwegian *Hop*), a narrow inlet; e.g., Longhope in Orkney.

seemed to say; he who sets himself up against me is in danger from that moment. His tongue was like a rasp: when it attacked a man it left him thin; and in his severity he took to putting the martial symbol after his name: N. Arentsen ♂. Oh, that rascal Nikolai the parish clerk's son, he was in such demand as was never seen. It was half a dollar to ask him the simplest question, a whole dollar for a piece of advice, and two dollars to have a paper drawn up. But he was sociable in his manners, he offered people a chair when they came into his office, and by no means insisted on being paid in silver, but was just as ready to take notes. If he met an acquaintance when he was taking a walk after office hours, fagged out with professional work, he was not too proud to say: "Come on, let's go to Sirilund and have a drink to the success of your case!"

Attorney Arentsen had seen tangible fruits of his visit to the neighbouring parish too. There was, for instance, Levion of Torpelvik; he was the neighbour of Marelius who had sold the Englishman fishing rights in the river. Was not Levion owner of the other bank of the same river, and ought not Sir Hugh to make it good to him in like manner? Did that infernal Englishman think he could fling away money to Marelius and no one else? Ah, but Marelius had a big grown-up daughter, that was where it was. . . . Marelius for his part did not hide the fact that he was dear friends with Sir Hugh, and even let on that he could *speaka Englisk* with him. And the daughter, the big grown-up Edvarda who was named after Edvarda Mack, she soon learned to talk this foreign English in private with the gentleman and understood him even when he whispered.

But Levion, he went to Attorney Arentsen and explained how matters stood. Arentsen nodded that he was right. He asked:

Benoni

"How broad is the river at its narrowest?"

"Some twelve fathoms by the waterfall. That's the narrowest."

"How long is the fishing-rod employed?"

Levion didn't understand this, but it was explained to him: if the Englishman had thrown his line beyond the middle of the stream they could get him beyond a doubt. And Levion began to hedge, to haggle with himself; at last he asserted that the river was never in this world more that eight fathoms across at the narrowest.

"Does Sir Hugh refuse to pay?"

"I don't know," replied Levion. "I haven't asked him."

"H'm. We'll summon him before the Conciliation Board."

Arentsen summoned him. Sir Hugh appeared and was all for peace and quietness; he offered to pay the same as he had paid Marelius. He mentioned the amount.

Levion only shook his head savagely and said:

"That's too little; you paid much more. And what about Edvarda getting new clothes, inside and out, where did she get them from?"

Sir Hugh got up and left the Conciliation Board.

"Now we'll summon him to the Sessions," said Attorney Arentsen.

"I'm thinking day and night about the great wrong that Marelius has done me," remarked Levion. "He's sold the salmon in the river and he's sold the salmon in the sea. Now the Englishman's been fishing from a boat right off my bit of shore."

Attorney Arentsen said:

"We'll summon Marelius as well."

Short and precise, with a look of determination the legal luminary made his decisions. This was no ordinary man. And when Levion came to pay and had nothing

Benoni

but miserable paper money, Arentsen took that too without any bother....

It was Sessions time at Sirilund.

Mack's housekeeper had sent Sven Watchman round the neighbourhood for poultry and all kinds of provisions; she had taken the under-miller's wife to help in the kitchen and there was no end to her preparations for the arrival of the authorities. She had also contrived that Rosa Barfod came and made herself useful and agreeable. The servants' hall was rigged up as the court-room, with a great cloth-covered table for the court and small tables for a lawyer or two. All around the tables was a bar. The clerk of the court had his office in the other end of the same building.

Oh, but it turned out a poor sort of Sessions.

The Governor did not come as he had written and said; the good housekeeper was bitterly disappointed over the absence of the principal authority. But, what was far worse, the District Judge did not come either. The elderly District Judge was prevented by ill-health and had to send his deputy. This man gave Mack himself immense food for thought; he inquired at once after the Judge.

He was indisposed, was not confined to his bed, but had lost weight, slept badly, seemed a prey to some kind of scruples.

What kind of scruples?

The deputy gave one or two examples: they had been used to this and that at the office, now it was thus and thus—in short, religious scruples.

"What, *that* man?"

The deputy said with dignity:

"The Judge asked me to convey to you his best thanks for a half-barrel of cloudberries you sent him last winter——"

Benoni

"Oh, a trifle!"

"——and regretted that he was unable to thank you in person."

Then Mack went to the window and looked out and thought. . . .

The Court was opened.

There sat the judge, the young deputy, with two clerks, at the cloth-covered table; on each side of him he had two jurors, chosen from the local good men and true. At their own little tables sat the attorney from town and Attorney N. Arentsen ♂, both with papers and books before them. If you looked carefully, the old town attorney had not so many papers as last year and fewer than Arentsen. Now and then a man came in and asked to have a word with one or other of the lawyers, and the greater number came to Arentsen.

Then one by one the different cases were taken: prosecutions, boundary disputes, lawsuits, registrations; Arentsen was in the thick of it the whole time, speaking, taking notes, dictating minutes. He might have been more impressed by the solemnity of the occasion, the young judge inspired no awe in him; nor did he address him as Judge like the others, but simply as Mr. Deputy. Arentsen laid a piece of evidence on the judges' table and said: "There you are, it's good enough to frame." In the case of Aron of the Hope, from whom a boat had been borrowed without leave, he said: "That is the law." To which the judge remarked, slightly huffed: "In general, yes; but here there is this and that to be considered." "That is the law," repeated Arentsen. And the public outside the bar nodded and thought: that fellow knows the law, it's grand to hear him.

On account of all Nikolai Arentsen's brand-new cases, the young judge could see no end to the Sessions this time. He toiled and drudged conscientiously, had wit-

Benoni

nesses examined, turned up records, read, wrote and spoke; but it was not till the third and last day that he reached the case of Levion of Torpelvik and Hugh Trevelyan.

Sir Hugh had been in attendance from the very first day, had hung about the place and strolled into the courtroom, without seeing or hearing anybody, with British rudeness, dumb even when people greeted him with "Peace!" He was quite sober. He took his meals at Mack's table and had a room in his house; but though he sat by the deputy judge at every meal, he never mentioned his case. In fact he hardly spoke at all.

"Now your case is coming on," the deputy said to him at dinner.

"Good," he answered unconcernedly.

He appeared with his fishing-rod, but without a lawyer, took off his cap with the salmon-flies in it, gave his name, title and domicile in England. To Arentsen's opening he added some brief statements which were taken down: that he had already offered before the Conciliation Board to pay Levion the same as Marelius, but that the sum he named had been called in question as too little.

"How much did Marelius receive?"

Sir Hugh mentioned the sum and added that Marelius was present and could give evidence.

Marelius gave his evidence on his "corporal oath" according to law.

The judge could not help remarking:

"But isn't that a handsome payment, Mr. Junior Attorney Arentsen?"

"But he don't say what Edvarda got besides," suddenly exclaimed Levion outside the bar.

"Silence!" ordered the judge.

Then Arentsen objected on behalf of his client:

Benoni

"But this is information which has a bearing on the case."

The judge asked a couple of questions and got a couple of answers; then he thought a moment and said:

"On what case has it a bearing? Not on the price of fishing rights."

Sir Hugh explained further: his opponent asserted that the river was only eight fathoms across at the narrowest and that in consequence he had been fishing at least as much on the wrong side. But the river was narrowest at the waterfall and there it was twelve fathoms across.

"Have you measured it?" Arentsen asked.

"Yes."

"And how long is your fishing-rod?"

"Two fathoms. Here it is."

Again Levion could not contain himself:

"I have measured the river, it's eight fathoms across at the waterfall."

"Silence!"

Arentsen assumed an air of astonishment and objected again:

"But the river falls in the summer months and that makes it only eight fathoms?"

The judge allowed Sir Hugh to stand down and asked Arentsen:

"Have you witnesses to prove that the river is only eight fathoms across at the waterfall?"

"No other witness than the owner."

"I ought to know my own waterfall," said Levion aloud.

A man outside the bar asked to be sworn to give evidence as to the breadth of the river: When the action was begun in the spring he measured the river at

Benoni

Marelius' request: it was a good thirteen fathoms at the waterfall. Two others among the public were sworn and gave the same evidence; all three were well-known local men. Two days before, they had again measured the river by request: it had not shrunk a full fathom, so it was still a good twelve fathoms.

There was, however, no expert among them; they measured the river and they measured the fishing-rod, but nothing was said about how far one could throw with a two-fathom rod. The young judge thought: Sir Hugh is not liable to pay even what he has offered. He sent for a yard measure from Mack's store simply for the sake of helping this stranger from a foreign land; his rod was measured and it was two fathoms.

The judge asked:

"Have you no witnesses at all, Mr. Junior Attorney?"

"Not on this point."

"Have you visited the spot in dispute?"

"I have relied on the owner's statement."

"Have you visited the spot?"

"No."

Everything was taken down, and at short intervals it was read over and approved. Things looked bad for Arentsen and his client, they whispered together, they consulted; then the attorney asked whether Sir Hugh was still willing to pay what he had offered before the Conciliation Board. In that case the terms would be accepted.

Sir Hugh answered No. He asked for judgment now.

Then Arentsen played his last card: But it appeared that Sir Hugh had been fishing lately east of the river mouth, in the sea, where Levion's proprietary right could not be contested.

Sir Hugh was called again. He did not quite understand: did they think he had been fishing in brackish water? His face writhed with contempt of such a low kind of fishing.

"Haven't you been fishing at the river mouth?"

No. What should he fish there for? There was no fish there yet. The salmon were still in the rivers and did not come down before autumn, after spawning.

'Oh, what a lot of natural history!" remarked Arentsen, dismissing the subject. "But are not salmon always to be found in the sea?"

"Yes, but you don't fish for them with a fly."

"Then what were you fishing for east of the river mouth?"

Sir Hugh would explain: he was fishing with a handline. He fished for codling and haddock. And it was not off the river mouth, it was several hundred fathoms from the shore, out at sea. The man who had rowed him every time was here present; it was the crofter whose cottage he had rented. He could give evidence.

The man was sworn and confirmed it all.

So Arentsen was obliged to ask for the adjournment of the case. . . .

But it was not the same old Sessions as before, far from it. When the District Judge presided in person, there was a chance even for people outside the bar to put a question to him on some point of law and get an answer; this young deputy was so afraid of having an answer coaxed out of him which might lead to complications. "The judge is not a solicitor," he said; "it's his business to give judgment; apply to a solicitor if you want information."

There was not a man among them who had a good word for this newfangled judge; people left the court and assembled round Mack's spirit counter, only those who had to stayed behind. So that when the mortgage deeds were read out by one of the clerks, there were only a few to listen to them. What they heard was no news either: that Benoni Hartvigsen had deposited five thousand dollars with Ferdinand Mack of Sirilund against a bond had been made no secret by Benoni himself, it was known to everybody. And it meant no more than when other people deposited their few dollars, only that Benoni's amount was so huge, oh, such a fortune!

When at last the Sessions were closed, the young judge was both tired and hungry; but he had taken so small a fancy to Attorney Arentsen on account of his unceremonious city tone, and he found his action against Hugh Trevelyan so flimsy and frivolous, that he might well have pronounced judgment at once and dismissed it there and then. And the complaint against Marelius of Torpelvik for having sold the fishing rights in another proprietor's share of the river might have been nonsuited.

Nikolai Arentsen said to his client:

"I intend to visit the spot myself and call witnesses. For that matter, there's only one court in Norway from which there is no appeal, and it isn't this one."

He went down to Mack's to find Rosa. He had not by any means come off a loser at these Sessions, so he had nothing to fret about. And in fact he walked with the steady, guaranteed carriage he had adopted since he began to be in great demand and to earn money like grass.

Rosa was in a long apron and ashamed to be seen. "Go into the little parlour a moment, I'll be there directly," she said.

She came just on his heels and said:

"I haven't much time. Are you all right? Is the court closed? How did you get on?"

"I got on finely of course. It is I who am the Law."

"Why hadn't I time to come and hear you!"

Aye, what lies Rosa could tell in her love for this man!

Benoni

She had watched her opportunity and both heard and seen him in court while his great case against Sir Hugh was on. And it pained her so much that that young deputy judge should be so impertinent as to ask twice running: Have you visited the spot? Have you visited the spot? Then she had stolen out of court again with grave misgivings. Thank Heaven, it meant nothing after all, Nikolai was sure to win all his cases.

"You remember the date, don't you?" she said.

"The date?"

"Our wedding-day. What I was going to say—— Oh!"

"Well?"

"We'll ride to church."

"Will we?"

"Yes, we'll ride to church. Now do you remember the date? The twelfth of June. It's not long till then."

"The twelfth of June," he repeated. "I'll make arrangements to be called in time."

"What nonsense you talk!" she said with an indulgent laugh.

He asked:

"The twelfth of June? But shan't we put up the banns?"

"They *have* been put up," she replied. "Papa did it at home and the curate here. Three times."

"Well, it's a good thing you saw to it. I have so much to do."

"Poor you! But then you're making a lot of money?"

"Like grass," he replied. . . .

The next day Sir Hugh returned to his cottage and his fishing. He went round by Benoni's houses and followed the rocks right up to the common; now and then he bent down and knocked off a little piece and put it in his pocket.

XVII

BENONI came home again from the outlying stations and began at once to fit out his seine. He had had no definite news of herring, but he made as if he knew a little more than other people; and really there was no staying at home for him, now that the whole country-side knew of his humiliation. The idea he had had of going to sea had died a natural death.

The Sheriff's officer came and told him about the Sessions and about the publication of the mortgage deed.

No, it was like a fate, it had been impossible for him to recover the document unpublished because it had already been entered in the great registry of mortgages before the Sessions came to Sirilund. So it had to take its course.

Benoni sat and listened in despair: then perhaps by his own act he had thrown away all Mack's good offices with Rosa. He was further given to understand that few people had been present to hear the publication, only the personnel of the Court and one or two more. It had passed off quietly.

"I have the document in my pocket, by the way," said the Sheriff's officer.

"Ah, you have," said Benoni, expecting to get it.

But the other was in no hurry, he sat still and coughed and pursed his lips.

"Was it dearer than we thought?" asked Benoni at last, quite ready to pay more.

"No, that was the full legal sum."

Benoni

Benoni waited a bit and said:

"Let me just take a little look at it."

The Sheriff's officer began:

"I could produce it this moment, but that would not be a proper thing to do. I wish to proceed like a human being."

Benoni stared at him and asked:

"You don't mean that! What's the matter with the document?"

At last the Sheriff's officer answered:

"The matter is that it's an inferior document. I will go so far as to say that it is not good enough for all your money."

"Let me see it this moment."

"If I wanted to proceed like a monster, I would lay it open before your eyes on the spot. But I'm preparing you gently for the news that Mack of Rosengaard has a thumping mortgage on Sirilund *before you.*"

"You're monkeying!" exclaimed Benoni in consternation.

At last the Sheriff's officer produced the bond. It stated that it had been duly registered on such and such a day. Then it was endorsed with all the previous mortgages on Sirilund and its appurtenances including the three vessels: it was Mack of Rosengaard who owned the whole lot and had owned it for many years; the total sum amounted to eighteen thousand dollars. The endorsement was signed Steen Thode.

It came upon Benoni like a stroke. He stared at these written words and began to fuss over trifles: Steen Thode was not the District Judge; who could he be? Eighteen thousand dollars, well, well; but then that Mack of Sirilund was no mighty man at all, it was his brother, Mack of Rosengaard, who owned him.

"Now the thing is whether the security you have got

Benoni

is worth as much as twenty-three thousand dollars," said the Sheriff's officer.

Benoni began to think.

"Oh, no," he said; "it's not."

"No, that's what the Sheriff and I think too; we've talked it over quietly. Twenty-three thousand, that's terrific."

"Is it lawful what Mack's done?"

"Now that depends. It says in the paper: received. Mack has received five thousand dollars against such-and-such security. I suppose you've accepted the security?"

Benoni was not listening to him any longer; he asked:

"Who's this fellow Steen Thode? Is it a lawful name?"

After an elaborate explanation the Sheriff's officer came to the conclusion that the deputy was lawful; but a District Judge he was not, far from it.

"Twenty-three thousand! Why, that Mack's a beggar," said Benoni suddenly. "It's much better to have a little less and own it yourself . . ." But all at once he remembered that his own five thousand must now be regarded as lost, and he got up, stood for a moment pale and bewildered, looking at the worthless paper on the table, and then sat down again.

"Of course it may be that he'll pay you little by little," said the Sheriff's officer to comfort him.

"Where is he to get it from? Why, he doesn't own the clothes on his back. It's much better to have a little less and . . . That Mack's a scoundrel, I believe."

"Now that's not a lawful thing to say. And it may be that he'll pay . . ."

"A scoundrel, that's just what he is!"

Oh, that name was good and strong. And there was something degrading to Mack's haughtiness in it which made Benoni use it so heartily.

Benoni

"I expect he'll pay," said the Sheriff's officer soothingly, and got up; he wanted a chance to be off.

But Benoni said in the utmost irritation:

"Nobody ought to have anything to do with him. The proper thing to do with a man like that is to spit him out of your mouth and say: so much for him!"

When Benoni was left alone, he considered awhile what steps he should take. He decided to go straight to Mack's office and settle accounts with him; he put the mortgage in his pocket and betook himself to Sirilund. On the way the idea occurred to him that he'd speak to Sven Watchman first.

But poor Sven Watchman was in a pretty bad way himself just now, not fit to cheer anyone up. It was Ellen Parlour-maid's fault again.

The evening before, Sven Watchman was standing having a little chat with his girl, when there was a call for her, Mack was going to have a bath. Sven Watchman tried to hold her back. "Let him have his bath by himself," he said; "what's it got to do with you?" But Ellen, she knew better and got away. Sven Watchman followed in his stocking feet and stood in the passage holding his breath and listened at Mack's door with both his ears.

This morning he got hold of Ellen Parlour-maid and said:

"Is Mack up?"

"No."

"You bathed him last night?"

"Well, I rubbed him over the back with a towel."

"That's a lie. I was in the passage and heard."

Pause.

"You all want me, the whole lot of you," said Ellen Parlour-maid quietly; "I think you're all crazy."

"Well, but can't you just give him the slip?"

"Not very well. You see, I've got to rub his back."

Sven Watchman's fury ran away with him, he blurted out with a snort:

"Oh, you're a swine, that's what you are."

She listened to him with staring eyes and eyebrows raised high; it looked as if she found Sven Watchman's abuse incredible.

"I shall have to stick a knife into you one of these days."

"There's no need for you to take on so," she said chattily. "He'll let me be right enough."

"No, he won't let you be."

"What about you and Bramaputra? Her with the frizzly hair," said Ellen with contempt.

Sven Watchman asked again:

"Is Mack up?"

"No."

"I'm going to have a talk to him in the office."

"You shouldn't do that," said Ellen, trying to dissuade him. "You'll only make trouble for both of us."

And probably it would have passed off quietly with him; but when Sven Watchman was put to drying the feather-bed out of Mack's bath in the sun, it made him uncommonly angry. He forgot that he was an odd-job man about the place and could be put to anything.

When Mack went into the office Sven Watchman followed, beside himself with excitement. He went straight to the point: his name was Sven Johan Kjeldsen and they called him Sven Watchman; he was to marry Ellen Parlour-maid; he'd see that she didn't bath Mack and he himself was not going to dry the feathers after them. . . . "Do you understand, she shan't be your swine, as sure as my name's Sven Johan Kjeldsen. For that's my name. And if you want to know my geography, I'm from town. Yes. That's where I come from, if you want to know."

Mack slowly looked up from his papers with steely eyes and asked:

"What was your name, did you say?"

Sven was confused, repeated the question and answered:

"What's my name? Sven Johan Kjeldsen. And as I told you, Sven Watchman."

"Good, now you can go to your work," said Mack.

Sven already had hold of the door-handle.

"No," he said, "I won't go to that work."

"Good, then you can take your wages."

Mack took up his quill pen and made a calculation, counted out the money and paid him. Then he opened the door.

And Sven Watchman growled, but went.

But when he was left with his handful of small coin and his despair, he slipped into the spirit counter and tossed off a few good drams. That made him so brave and strong. He stormed into the servants' hall and fell foul of the other men, broke in on the two ancients, Fredrick Mensa and Mons, who now lay in bed, both of them, taking nourishment and uttering a word or two just as if they were human.

"You two have got to get up and chop wood," said Sven Watchman to them; "I've finished."

"Finished," said Fredrick Mensa.

"Hold your jaw!" shrieked Sven Watchman. "Will you get up? Do you want poor Ellen to go out to the wood-shed again?"

Fredrik Mensa was lying with scraps of food and spittle in his beard; he thought gravely about something and blinked his eyes, then he said:

"Three mile to Funtus."

and say: O, ye Sorosi lasses! You do nothing but dance, you're just like a lot of animals."

An urgent message from Mack called the foreman of the farm-hands to the office. At once a feeling of constraint came over the servants' hall and one after another left it; it was beyond the power of Sven Watchman to put any life into them again. Then the under-miller's wife sent her little boy up to him to say good-bye nicely and thank him once more for the present. Sven kept hold of his little hand a long time and said: "I declare it's almost the same as holding Ellen's hand; did you ever know the like!"

Then there was a call for Sven Watchman himself and he went with heavy forebodings. Oh, but it was only Benoni, who was out in the yard and wanted a word with him.

"It's only a little thing I want to ask you," said Benoni by way of an opening; "it's whether you'll take a hand in the seining."

"I don't know. Yes, I will. The seining?"

But soon they began to talk about what was really on the minds of both, and Benoni nodded threateningly: he intended to go and see Mack in the office.

"I've already been there to-day and told him what I think of him."

"For he's treated me so shamefully."

"What about me? Ellen's no longer fit for any mortal soul."

"How's that?"

"He had her to bath him again last night."

"And got hold of her?" . . . Benoni shook his head; there was nothing to be done about that.

"But now you see it's this way: Ellen and I are going to get married," said Sven Watchman.

Benoni answered:

Benoni

"You won't get her till afterwards, you know that well enough."

Sven Watchman looked up ominously.

"It's the rule," said Benoni. "It's been like that with one of them after the other. But Bramaputra, she was the only one that took it much to heart."

The foreman returned from Mack and announced that Sven Watchman was to leave the premises.

"Leave——? What——?"

"That's the orders. It's my place to be in charge and see to everything here, so that's all I can say."

Sven Watchman may have had in his mind some way of making his peace for Ellen's sake; now he saw that he would have to go and it took away all his spirit.

Benoni interposed:

"You can go back and tell him that Sven Watchman is coming to me."

"Oh, all right," answered the foreman.

"You can say that to Mack of Sirilund from Benoni Hartvigsen."

The foreman went. The two were left feeling good and proud over the high tone they had taken. But as their talk went on, Sven Watchman's spirits sank again at the idea of leaving Sirilund.

"I've nothing left in the world but a diamond," said he. "But I haven't any glass to cut with it."

While they were standing there, Mack himself came down the steps of the store and made straight for them, walking at his natural pace. When he was near enough, they both touched their hats.

"What sort of a message was that you sent me?" asked Mack.

"Message? Oh, it was only something I said," answered Benoni, a little shaken.

"Are you still here?" Mack asked the other.

Benoni

Sven Watchman held his tongue.

But now Benoni had had a little time, a second or two, and he drew himself up. Wasn't he part-owner of Sirilund? And wasn't he face to face with a poverty-stricken scoundrel?

"What do you want to come and catechize us for?" he asked, looking Mack in the face.

The two men took each other's measure with great hostility; but Benoni was only a beginner. Mack took out his cambric handkerchief and made a show of using it; then he turned to Sven Watchman and said:

"Haven't you been told to go?"

And Sven Watchman took himself off.

"You go home to my place," Benoni called after him. "Here's the key; I dare trust you with all my worldly goods. Just you go in and wait for me; I've got to have a word or two with this man."

"This man," of Mack of Sirilund!

They went into the office; Mack used his handkerchief again and said:

"Well?"

"It's only a small matter," replied Benoni; "It's about the money."

"What about the money?"

"You've defrauded me."

Mack said nothing and looked indulgent.

"For now I've had the mortgage deed registered. You didn't think I was up to that?"

Mack's mouth showed a smile:

"Oh, yes, I knew all about it."

"It's your brother at Rosengaard that owns you, lock, stock and barrel. See here . . ." Benoni took out the deed and pointed.

"What's the meaning of this?" asked Mack. "Do you want to call in your money?"

Benoni

"Call in my money? Where are you to get it from? You don't own the town shoes you stand in. Twenty-three thousand; your brother has eighteen and I five, that makes twenty-three. You've ruined me, I'm almost as big a pauper as yourself."

Mack answered:

"In the first place, it's only a young deputy who wrote all that on your bond."

"Well, he's lawful."

"No doubt. But the Judge would not have endorsed it with all this nonsense about my brother. It's only a matter of form, you know, between brothers. As a matter of fact, I have backed my brother oftener than he has me—when he was extending his fish-glue factory, for instance."

"Ah, yes, you're one as bankrupt as the other, I expect. But that don't make it any better for me."

"In the second place," Mack continued with undisturbed loftiness, "it is not five thousand that I owe you. We have an account outstanding."

"You mean the four hundred for the heirlooms? But what am I to do with those heirlooms? Rosa and the Attorney have had their banns asked, they're to be married on the twelfth."

"I don't know how it was, I couldn't get Rosa to change her mind; but it is not impossible that you were partly to blame. That publication behind my back did not exactly encourage me to take your part."

"What of it?" cried Benoni with irritation. "Pleasant journey to Rosa; I'm not going down on my knees to her. But when you think of all your rascal's tricks, why, Rosa's too good to be your goddaughter. Yes. And I'll write her a letter and tell her never to cross your threshold again. Account outstanding. I won't have any account outstanding with you, I"ll try and pay cash

Benoni

for the heirlooms as soon as ever I can. Now let me have my five thousand."

"So you give notice of withdrawal at six months from date?"

"Give notice!" sneered Benoni. "No, I'm going to act very different. I'm not going to spare you and all your glory."

Mack saw very well that Benoni now had the upper hand and could bring him to his knees: he might declare him bankrupt, he might proceed against him and make trouble over the bond, damage his reputation, make his financial difficulties common talk.

"You may act in any way you please," he said coldly.

But Benoni was not equal to holding back his trump card, he played it out:

"I shall seize your dried fish out on the rocks yonder."

That would anyhow create a scandal, there would be an action, witnesses would be called. Mack answered:

"That fish is not mine. It belongs to the merchant."

Then Benoni was positively astounded and clutched at his shock of hair:

"But don't you possess anything in this world!"

"I don't owe you any information as to that," Mack replied, putting him down. "What you have a claim to is your money, and that you shall have. So you give six months' notice of withdrawal?"

And to end the matter Benoni said Yes.

Mack took his pen and made a note of the date. When he had finished he laid his pen down, looked at Benoni and said:

"I never thought it would end like this between us, Hartvigsen."

Benoni was not exactly pleased either when it came to the point:

"What would you have me do? Once I was down and

Benoni

couldn't look after myself, I know that very well. But granted it was you that raised me up from the dust . . ."

"I make no allusion to that," Mack interrupted. "It is you yourself who bring that in . . ." And Mack went to the window to think.

But now his miserable past actually appeared to Benoni in a very clear light; he thought of the days when he had no mansion and no boat-house or seine, the days when his humiliation was published at the church door and when Mack of Sirilund took him up and made a man of him again. He said in a tone of depression:

"Well, well, if I get my money, all right. I'm not going to act like a wolf to you. I haven't any reason to either, none at all."

Pause. Mack turned round and went back to his desk.

"Did you hear of any herring while you were away?"

Benoni answered:

"No. Oh, herring—yes, I heard of some, but no quantity. I've decided to go out with the seine again."

"Good luck!"

"Peace be with you!" said Benoni as he went out.

XVIII

IT is the twelfth of June, to-day Rosa is to be married. Well, well.

From early morn Benoni went about in a solemn frame of mind, was on his best behaviour, meek and mild. Sven Watchman, who was living in his house, was given a job which he could manage by himself without help.

Benoni polished the instrument and the silver. Should he send the heirlooms to Rosa? He no longer had a use for them himself. And then it would be like the sort of rich presents a king might send to a queen and it would stop the mouths of all the people who were actively spreading reports that Benoni Hartvigsen was bankrupt. For, to begin with, neither Benoni himself nor the Sheriff's officer had made any secret of the worthless mortgage of five thousand dollars, and now rumour was busy with him, magnifying the disaster and reckoning even the boathouse and the seine outfit as lost. Benoni's suspicions were reawakened; it seemed to him that his former cronies were inclined to treat him in the old free and easy fashion and had dropped calling him Hartvigsen. Oh, but he could very well afford to present Rosa with the heirlooms.

Would she accept them?

At any rate he might send her the silver. With fond sentimentality he pictured to himself how this grand gift would bring tears to Rosa's eyes: O Benoni, I repent that I did not take you instead! Why, she hadn't sent him back the ring and the cross either, as she said she would, so perhaps she wanted to keep them for love of him. Couldn't he at any rate send her the spoon and fork that he had laid aside for her and wrapped in a special paper?

No, she was not likely to accept anything.

Benoni drifted down to Sirilund, mournful and sore distressed, drank a lot of spirits at the store on the pretext of a turn of sickness, and went home again. Rather drunk, he took out his hymn-book for a godly purpose; but, as he was afraid Sven Watchman might hear his powerful singing, he had to content himself with *reading* the hymns, which bored him. He stood awhile in the closed veranda, looking out; but whether he looked through the yellow glass or the blue or the red, the doves were there performing the least of their tricks all over the boat-house wall. Oh, he had had such very different thoughts when he got the coloured glass and the doves for Rosa. . . .

He wandered over the rocks. A little way in front of him walked Schöning the lightkeeper, shabby and bent, as though shrunken with too much poverty. He was taking a stroll on the rocks and listening to the sea-gulls and looking at the sparse vegetation; contrary to his habit, he greeted Benoni and began to chat.

"Look here, Hartvigsen, you have the means, you ought to buy these rocks," he said.

"Ought I? I have rocks enough already," answered Benoni.

"No, you don't own nearly enough. You ought to buy the whole mile of them, up to the edge of the common."

"What should I do with them?"

"They're worth a lot of money."

"Are they worth a lot of money?"

"They're full of lead ore inside."

Benoni

"What then? Ore!" said Benoni scornfully.

"Yes, ore. Ore for a million. But, besides that, the ore is full of silver."

Benoni looked at the Lightkeeper and did not believe him.

"Why don't you buy them yourself?"

The Lightkeeper gave a withered smile and gazed into space.

"In the first place, I have not the means; in the second, I have no use for them. But you ought to do it, you have your life before you."

"Oh, you're not so old as that."

"Perhaps not. But what do I want with more than I have? I've been made keeper of a lighthouse of the fourth class, that's just enough for us to keep body and soul together; we can't eat more than we do."

Suddenly Benoni asked:

"Have you spoken to Mack about this?"

And the Lightkeeper with fine scorn answered but two words:

"To Mack?"

Then he turned and walked back across the rocks.

As Benoni went the opposite way he thought to himself: it's not a bad thing that the rocks are full of ore inside; it's Aron of the Hope that owns them; he's gone to law with a fisherman in the skerries for borrowing a boat without leave, and it costs money to go to law: the other day he took one of his cows to the Attorney. Well, well, that Nikolai's getting married to-day, so he'll want the cow, he and Rosa.

Benoni was overcome by memories of Rosa. He had come into the road over the common; his eyes grew moist, he could not see where he was going and flung himself down by the roadside. . . . Haven't I behaved as I ought to? tell me that. Didn't I, generally speaking, handle you

Benoni

lightly and gingerly when I took hold of you, so as not to hurt? Oh, God have mercy upon me!

"*Borre ækked!*"

Now Gilbert the Lapp is there again. He travels busily backwards and forwards across the common like a weaver's shuttle and leaves shreds of his clothes in the bushes on both sides of the mountain.

"I was just sitting here and taking a rest," said Benoni, feeling foolish. "It's nice to listen to the aspens."

"I've just come from a wedding," said Gilbert. "I met some folks we know," said he.

"Perhaps you were at the church?" asked Benoni.

"I was at the church. Grand wedding. That Mack was there too."

"Aye, he would be there."

"First came the bridegroom. On horseback."

"On horseback?"

"Then came the bride. On horseback."

Benoni wagged his head, that was doing it in style.

"She had a white veil nearly down to the ground."

Benoni was lost in thought. There, it was done now. A white veil, aye, aye. . . . Then he got up and walked homeward with Gilbert the Lapp. . . . "Aye, aye, that Benoni and I'll have to get over it!" he said. "Come in along with me a minute."

"Thanks, there's no call for me to be taking up your time."

When Benoni produced spirits and offered a dram, Gilbert said:

"You don't need to be so free-handed!"

"You shall have a drink for your great news," says Benoni with trembling lips. "And a pleasant journey to her!" he says.

Gilbert drinks and his eyes wander about the room; he expresses his surprise that certain people don't care to

Benoni

live in a room like this where there is every kind of riches. To this, Benoni answers that Oh, yes, he's about as well off as a poor man can be. And he shows Gilbert the piano and explains that it's an instrument, he shows him the work-table inlaid with ebony and silver, and then he tops all by bringing out the silver. "That cost me a hundred dollars," says he.

Gilbert wags his head awhile, and again he can't understand why certain people would thrust away the like of that. At last he says:

"She didn't look happy in church."

"Rosa? Didn't she?"

"No. It was just as if she repented what she was doing."

Benoni got up, stood right in front of Gilbert and said:

"You see this ring? It shall no longer stay upon my hand to bring me vexation of spirit." . . . He took the ring off his right hand and put it on his left with these words: "Did you see what I did?"

Gilbert solemnly answered: "Yes."

Then Benoni fetched the almanac and said:

"You see that mark? Now I cross it out. It's Sylverius's Day I've crossed out."

"Sylverius's Day," repeated Gilbert.

"You are my witness," said Benoni.

When that was done he had nothing left to be solemn about and lapsed into silence. . . .

Gilbert went to the store at Sirilund and told the story of the wedding, how nobody could have seen anything finer, how the white veil swept the ground, how the bride had got the man of her choice and looked happy. And how that Mack himself was in church.

When Gilbert the Lapp had finished at Sirilund, he strolled for a while on the road to the parish clerk's. The newly married couple arrived as evening was drawing on;

Benoni

Rosa was still on horseback, but Young Arentsen had got sore from the saddle and trudged distressfully on foot leading his horse by the bridle. It was a bright evening and warm weather, the sun was still up, but the seabirds had gone to rest.

Gilbert pulled off his cap to the bridal couple. Rosa rode on, but Young Arentsen stopped and gave his horse to Gilbert. He was tired and in a vile temper.

"Here, take the beast and tether it somewhere. I've towed it long enough."

"I was in church and saw you," said Gilbert.

Young Arentsen answered savagely:

"I was in church too, looking on at the wedding. I hadn't a chance to slip away."

Thus Rosa and Young Arentsen made their entry into the parish clerk's house where they were to live. . . .

A few days after, Benoni went out with the big seine and all his crew. Such confidence was there in his luck that more hands had offered than he wanted. Sven Watchman sailed as an extra hand in the pay of the owner.

XIX

THE sun stood high and shone endlessly, hour after hour, day and night. Young Arentsen through his long absence from home had grown unused to all this sunshine at night, he began to lose his sleep and could not get the room dark enough. To make things worse, his father, the old parish clerk, lay ill in a room across the passage, and the son could easily hear him groaning faintly, though there was the passage between. He got up, put on his clothes and went out. And Rosa still lay sleeping soundly and undisturbed, with only a sheet over her in the warm summer night.

And now that the haymaking was on, the Attorney hadn't such an overwhelming mass of business as earlier in the year. At the beginning he had made use of Rosa to help him with all the long and tiresome writing; now he could get through the work alone, there was no more than that; since the Sessions he had had nothing but a few conciliation summonses to put through. But all the big cases that had not been settled at the Sessions were now travelling round from one judge to another and automatically serving the turn of Attorney Arentsen, while he himself took it easy and now and then found an excuse for visiting Mack's spirit counter.

Judgment had been given in the case of Hugh Trevelyan and Levion of Torpelvik. It had cost Arentsen a great effort. On his way across the mountain to his own wedding, he had had to make a big detour to visit the disputed site of the famous salmon-fishing and measure the stream

Benoni

by the waterfall. He had two men with him. On seeing Sir Hugh standing there fishing from the opposite bank, he greeted him as an acquaintance and took off his hat; but the good Englishman remained stolidly British and did not acknowledge his greeting. If Rosa had been there, she would have been vexed. Furious at the snub, Arentsen gave his men orders to be close in their measurements; but the river was still only twelve fathoms across.

"I don't care what the breadth is," said Arentsen. He had been watching Sir Hugh and, measuring simply by the eye, had convinced himself that the angler's fly actually fell nearer to Levion's bank than to Marelius'. He called the two men to witness this and got a written declaration from them. Then he added a rider to his first statement and posted it.

And now judgment had been given, his visit to the spot had been wasted labour: Sir Hugh was declared liable to pay what he had himself offered before the Conciliation Board and not a penny more.

When Sir Hugh had received the judgment, he came with witnesses and again offered payment: here's your money! But once more the affair came to grief over Levion's greediness. "You have got the fishing rights too cheap because you've been paying Edvarda separate," said he; "she's just put in five and twenty dollars at Mack's." Sir Hugh offered the money once again, was refused and left.

But the case was by no means lost through this little judgment of the court of first instance. Sir Hugh's salmon-fishing was still an object of litigation with plenty of life in it. And the end of it was that it was to be brought before the Court of Appeal at Trondhjem; Attorney Arentsen would write a smashing plea in which the important factor of Sir Hugh's relations with the defendant's daughter would be duly shown up.

Benoni

"But this will necessitate some preliminary expenses," said Arentsen.

"I was afraid so. How much is it this time?"

"Four dollars this time."

"It's going to cost me dear to get my rights of the scoundrels."

"One's rights are never too dear," replied Arentsen.

Levion of Torpelvik paid and went.

Next!

Aron of the Hope. His case, to begin with, was nothing but a foolish prank: a young fisherman from the skerries had borrowed Aron's four-oared boat one night and kept it for two days. Where had he been those two days? With a girl. When the fisher-lad came back with the boat, Aron had met him with a threat of the new lawyer at the parish clerk's. The boy was greatly surprised; borrowing a boat without leave was such a common thing everywhere that he was inclined to treat Aron's threat as a joke. The end of it was that the boy declared: "I don't give a damn for you or your lawyer, so now you know it!" So Arentsen got the case. Oh, what a lot it was costing Aron of the Hope! One cow he had already brought to the parish clerk's in the middle of the summer when she was full of milk; at this rate he'd have to bring the next one to the slaughter by autumn.

"We can't drop this case," said Arentsen when it was lost in the little petty court of first instance; "I'm going to write a smashing plea for the Court of Appeal. But that will necessitate some preliminary expenses."

"Aye, expenses and expenses!" replied Aron testily. "I shan't be left with anything to live on soon."

"It can't be so bad as all that."

"Couldn't you get rid of the rocks for me?" asked Aron.

Benoni

"Rocks?"

"They say they'll be worth a lot of money some day. The Professor in Christiania has looked into it and written that it's lead ore with silver in it."

Attorney Arentsen replied:

"I haven't any use for the ore. But I never refuse silver, Aron."

So Aron of the Hope saw that his next cow was lost, and he signed a paper to that effect before leaving.

But even before the summer was over, Nikolai Arentsen was getting so bored that he began to talk about applying for a post as fishery magistrate for the coming Lofoten season. What was he to do at home in the winter? Nothing but women and children wherever you went, and not a shilling to be raised anywhere. Rosa made no objection to this, though perhaps she thought a newly married man might have hit upon something more reasonable than leaving his home at the first opportunity. Rosa took a hand and gave her help with one thing and another and had charge of the invalid parish clerk. The old man got gradually thinner and feebler and was now only waiting for dissolution; the schoolmaster had taken over all his duties. . . .

A change had taken place at Sirilund in that the ancient Mons had moved from his little bed to the churchyard. They found him one day lying as usual with a bit of food in his hand and a full-fed look about his mouth. Mons had not shown much sign of life for some years, so it was a little difficult to find out whether he was altogether extinct; and when they asked Fredrik Mensa in the other bed: "Do you think Mons is only asleep?" Fredrik Mensa answered in his usual way: "Asleep?" So they let Mons lie till next morning. But as he still hadn't eaten the bit of food, he was certainly dead. Fredrik Mensa witnessed from his bed the removal of his old

Benoni

mate; it did not concern him particularly, but still he joined in with human word or two which those present were able to comprehend: *"Kra, kra,* says the crow. Dinner? Ha-ha.". . .

Autumn was already coming on, the aspens were turning yellow, Mack's fish was dried and Arn Drier had sailed it away to Bergen in the schooner. The spawning salmon in the river had shrunk away to nothing, their summer gambols were over and Sir Hugh Trevelyan had packed his rod and gone home to England. He had promised the Torpelvik folk and promised Edvarda that he would come back in the spring. . . . And now they were cutting the corn and beginning to dig the potatoes on those farms that had had plenty of noonday sun during the summer.

And Benoni came home again with the big seine and all his crew. He had made no shot. However, as he was lying out in a good place for herring, Benoni would have chosen to stick to it for a few weeks so as to be on the spot when the winter herring arrived; but this would mean struggling through an expensive time for the owner who had a man in his pay into the bargain, besides which the crew were running short of funds and could not lie out there waiting. So Benoni sailed home again, a prey to that low-spirited feeling in his head.

The only one who kept up his spirits was Sven Watchman. Nor had he any cause to repine: he had drawn his wages all the summer while the rest had only been paying out, and now he had the added pleasure of returning to scenes dear to his heart. The very first evening he hurried to Sirilund, got hold of Ellen Parlour-maid on the sly and had a long and thrilling talk with her. For her sake he was ready to go to Mack and stand before him and ask to be allowed to stay. What would Mack answer?

Benoni

"If Mons is dead and Fredrik Mensa bedridden, I suppose you have to go to the shed and chop wood?" Sven Watchman asked his girl.

"Well, I can't say I don't."

"H'm. I suppose he still takes his baths?"

Ellen Parlour-maid gave a little wriggle.

"His baths? Yes."

"Then perhaps he's going to have another bath soon?"

"I don't know. Oh, yes, this evening."

"I can't stop any longer with Hartvigsen," Sven Watchman then said. "I've been drawing wages all summer and he's so cruel vexed we haven't had a shot."

"They say he's a poor man now," remarked Ellen.

To this Sven Watchman replied with indignation:

"Then it's a lie, whoever said it. A dirty scoundrelly lie any day of the week. Hartvigsen is a rich man when he gets his money back in a few months."

"Well, well," was all Ellen said to all this hastiness.

And in fact Sven too had but one thing in his head:

"So it all depends on whether I can be taken on here again," he said. "Can't you ask Mack?"

"I don't know. Do you think it would do?"

"Why shouldn't it do? When you bath him this evening? You see, I . . . It's this way, I'm quite happy here. And if I went aboard the mail-boat I'd only have to go ashore again. There's something strange about it, I don't know. . . . Let me feel your hands."

Her slender hands were like a child's, the fingers seemed hungry and powerless; oh, they were just made for Sven Watchman to bury in his big kindly fists. Then he drew her to him, lifted her on his arm, set her down again and gave her a long kiss. And did the same over again. "And, Ellen, I told you that more than once in the summer" said he.

"Talk to him this evening when you're bathing him,"

he went on; "when you're rubbing his back. Say that I've come back here, that I'm out of a job, and besides, who's to chop the wood? You know him well enough to do that: only take care you say it at the right time and don't make him riled. Ellen, it's a shame you have to ask him, but what are we to do?"

"I'll try and ask him this evening," she answered. . . .

A few days later Benoni walked over to Sirilund and met Sven Watchman. Benoni said:

"You had no call to leave me. I've been wanting you all the time for all sorts of jobs," he said with an important air: "Can't you come and sweep my kitchen chimney some time?"

"Yes, any day and hour you like."

"You see, my servant keeps up such a blaze with all her cooking that the flues get choked up. Are you going to stay here?"

Sven Watchman nodded that that was what it had come to. Mack had lent an ear to his request and thought awhile and finally said: You can stay.

"It's just as if there was witchcraft in it," said Benoni. "Haven't I been wanting you all the time? And haven't I plenty of things to be painted again?" he said, bragging away. "Do you expect me to go and daub away myself?"

Benoni had good cause for annoyance. No sooner had the touchy fellow come home again than he became aware that everybody looked upon him as ruined. They were sorry for it, Benoni had never been anything of an awkward neighbour or one to whom people turned in vain. But now he had lost his wealth and there was talk that he had mortgaged his buildings. On the top of all this his fishing luck had deserted him: not a shot the whole summer. Benoni was filled with great wrath every time the people of the place relapsed into their old trick of calling him plain Benoni. Steen the store clerk, who had a grudge

Benoni

against him since last Christmas, began to treat him bluntly as a brother.

"Who are you talking to like that?" asked Benoni indignantly. "You'd better not do it again."

"And you'd better not try and look like a cow when you're only a calf," retorted Steen the store clerk. Oh, that Steen, his sharp tongue was never at a loss.

"I shouldn't be surprised if that Mack'll have a word to say to you presently," Benoni threatened.

He went into Mack's office.

There stood Mack precisely as before, with his diamond pin in his shirt-front and his dyed hair and beard; no disaster had befallen his appearance. While rumour had buffeted Benoni so sorely, it had in no way shaken Mack of Sirilund, that proud patrician. He had appropriated Benoni's money to his own use—well, there, he was a slippery eel in business and didn't say No to five thousand dollars. But had anyone heard of his doing a fisherman's family out of their halfpence? He was not that sort.

"Well," said Mack to Benoni, "you had no luck this year?"

"No."

"One can't expect to be lucky every time."

"If only I had all the herring I came across on the way! But it was not so ordained that I should get it."

"You'll do better next time."

"I'd been making so sure you'd have waited till I came home before you shipped the fish to Bergen," said Benoni.

Mack replied:

"I really did not know when you were coming home. You might have sent me a letter."

"Oh, I dare say it was best to let that Arn Drier sail the schooner. He can do it so much better than me. Only it's what I had in my mind, you see, not that that's of any consequence."

Benoni

"If I had known when you were coming . . . But, for that matter, I was under no obligation to wait for you," said Mack curtly.

Benoni grew more subdued and began to talk about the outstanding account. This big creditor explained that he had earned nothing the whole summer, so he couldn't pay for the heirlooms. He stood there in preternatural humility and asked for time.

"I'm not dunning you," said Mack.

"Then it'll have to stand over till you pay me the five thousand," Benoni declared with a lingering trace of opulence.

"As you please. However, I am quite willing to take back the old treasures," Mack offered.

"Take them back?"

"At the same price. I miss the things."

Benoni pondered a moment. How could such a broken man as Mack make an offer like that? And what would folk say if Benoni let the heirlooms go out of his house? He was forced to do it, that's what they would say.

"At any rate I must have a piano and some more silver," said Mack.

"I don't know, I don't think I'm so hard up as to sell my things," Benoni said to that.

"As you please."

Mack nodded and took up his pen.

And Benoni walked homeward. Thank God, he was not yet in such distress that he had to ask Mack for credit at the store; hadn't he a bag of ready money hidden away in his chest, perhaps quite as much as Mack himself had in his cash-box? Then why the devil did people go and make up all these lies about him? He was comfortably off for food and housing, he-he, didn't go short of anything. And Mack in all his glory couldn't be so very substantial either, for all his talk about buying himself a

Benoni

new instrument and new silver; where was Mack to find the means for that? And Benoni's thoughts ran on Mack and he rated him as a great scoundrel with whom he would have nothing to do. And now he hadn't engaged Benoni either to sail the schooner to Lofoten next trip and buy cargo for the three vessels. So no doubt Arn Drier was to do that. . . .

Some weeks went by. Once more Benoni had nothing to do but go to church on Sundays.

XX

IT is a great pig-killing day at Sirilund. The young porker is already a corpse, and they are scalding it in boiling water; now it is the turn of the yearling hog, a piebald monster with rings in its snout. It takes a lot of men and women, this job of work: the foreman of the farm-hands is the one who does the sticking, Sven Watchman and Man Ole help at it, while the cook and Bramaputra run backwards and forwards for boiling water. They get no help from the dairymaid, she does nothing but weep for the animals; that has been her way all these years.

He's a little bit afraid of the big beast they have to tackle, is the foreman. Sven Watchman advised shooting him, as all decent people do; but the housekeeper put her foot down about this, because of the blood which she wouldn't be done out of.

"Come on, let's go and get him," says the foreman, plucking up courage.

"All right," answers Sven Watchman, and "All right," answers Man Ole.

They leave the womenfolk, who are still busy scalding and pulling the bristles out of the young pig's corpse. They are surrounded by a huge flock of crows and magpies cawing and making a terrible din.

The three men go to the pig-sty; the hog sticks his snout in the air and grunts and looks at them. They have a running noose ready to slip over his shoulders; the dairymaid entices the pig out into the yard with some food in a wooden bowl; he follows willingly enough, grunting as though to ask a question or two. The foreman calls out to Bramaputra to have the basin ready to catch the blood. Gently, halting now and again, the procession moves away to a sledge which had been put there for the slaughtering; now they have reached it. The cook leaves her work on the young pig and bolts into the kitchen, she can't stand the sight of blood: a shower of strong language follows her. Bramaputra is left standing with her basin; a fistful of salt has been thrown into the bottom of it. All is ready.

The hog takes turns at grunting a little and stopping to listen for a bit. He blinks his eyes and tries to understand what these humans are saying. The dairymaid has orders to stand by so as to quiet him, but she can see nothing for tears—and then all at once she runs away, howling and bent double, torn to pieces with grief. The hog gets out of hand at once and makes after her. "Put down the bowl if you can't do anything else, you blasted fool!" thunders the foreman; he was nervous enough before. But the dairymaid hears nothing.

Now the hog has started shrieking; he has this rope around his shoulders which keeps him from following the dairymaid and her bowl. What's the idea of these humans with this rope? He shrieks with all his might and the foreman has to shout his orders: "Don't let go the rope, damn you! There, that's done it! Oh, you devil!" he foams at Man Ole, who has let go his hold. The hog gallops across the yard, Sven Watchman is after him, catches the rope and pulls it taut: the huge mountain of pork rolls over. Sven Watchman himself gets a jerk, but keeps his feet by a miracle.

In a dangerous rage the foreman puts down his long knife and goes up to Man Ole:

"I reckon you were looking at the crows when you let go, weren't you?"

Benoni

"What's it got to do with you? Are they your crows?"

"Oh, that's the way of it!" The foreman is absolutely furious. Hadn't he gone and picked his men for this hazardous job? He went to Sven Watchman and said:

"You'll have to help kill a pig or two to-day." And he said to Man Ole: "you'll have to come too."

Now he gives three quiet shakes to his fist and asks in the accents of a man:

"Do you see this?"

But Man Ole only laughs at him and says:

"Not even the magpies are yours."

"This here," says the foreman, alluding to his fist, "this here I'm going to plant in your dial if you let go again."

"Oh, get away. Let me have the knife and I'll soon do for the pig."

"*You?*"

Sven Watchman comes back hauling the hog, which is still shrieking and struggling violently. Then Man Ole spits first in one hand and then in the other and takes hold of the rope again. Sven Watchman has another noose ready to slip over the pig's snout; he stands watching his chance.

"Look out!" cries Bramaputra. . . . She knows it's a dangerous job he has; the hog may make a dash at his hand and tear it if he's too rash.

"If you don't let that Sven Watchman alone now!" the foreman warns her with suppressed fury. He is jumping with excitement.

Bramaputra gives him a look.

"I wouldn't kiss you, you're in such a temper," she answers.

Man Ole's eyes shrink to sharp points when he hears this.

"I'll plug your jaw for you," he threatens.

Benoni

Sven Watchman has made his first cast round the pig's snout and follows it up with others, quick as lightning. Now the animal is harmless and can be handled; its shrieks are stifled, it breathes with difficulty through its tied-up muzzle. Then the hog is seized by the four legs and hoisted on to the sledge. The men's grip from sheer nervousness and excitement is so needlessly adamantine and invincible, and the animal lies completely overpowered on the sledge. The foreman reaches for his knife and begins to take aim.

"Not too high up," Man Ole advises him.

"Don't speak to him now," warns Bramaputra, stirring the salt in her basin. It gives a scraping sound.

Then the knife goes in. The foreman gives it a couple of digs to get through the tough skin, and then the long knife seems to melt into the fat throat right up to the haft.

At first the hog doesn't notice anything; he lies for a few seconds and thinks a bit. But then he knows he has been killed and squeals out his stifled cries until he can do no more. All the time the blood has been gushing out of his throat and Bramaputra stirs her basin incessantly. . . .

"It's an easy death to be killed," said Sven Watchman thoughtfully.

"Perhaps you've tried it?"

"It don't last more than a minute for the one who sticks or the one who dies." . . .

Sven Watchman took the afternoon off to go to Benoni's house and sweep the chimney. He had armed himself with long birch-rods and a sprig of juniper on a thick piece of wire.

Benoni was at home. It was only one of his queer foolish whims having his chimney swept; it was simply and solely to show people that the chimney of his house was much used and the kitchen fire hardly ever out.

Benoni

"I'm sure you deserve my best thanks for doing me this favour," said Benoni as he poured out a drink for Sven Watchman. The friendship between these two was unbroken, because Sven Watchman was always so civil in his manners.

"I should think it a shame if I wouldn't do Hartvigsen a little favour," he replied.

He went out into the kitchen, cleared the range of pots and pans and then proceeded to the roof. Benoni followed him out of doors and stood below talking to him:

"How do you find the soot, is it greasy?"

"Just so," answered Sven, "greasy and shiny."

"Yes, that's the smoke of the roast joints," said Benoni. "I keep on telling my cook we can get along without all this high living, but . . ."

"Ah, you may talk to a woman!" said Sven with a bantering laugh.

"Oh, well, poor thing, she's got into the way of it in my house," Benoni excused her. "The soot's greasy and black, you say?"

"It's the blackest and greasiest soot ever I saw."

Benoni was extremely well pleased with himself and delighted in the company of his old shipmate of the *Funtus* and the seine-boat. He did all he could to keep Sven happily employed up on the roof so that the people going to and from the store at Sirilund might have a good view of him.

"I reckon I'll buy that diamond of yours," he said.

"That's too much altogether. And what would you do with it?"

"It can just lie there. I don't know how it is, I'm getting such a lot of treasures. The place'll soon be stacked with them from floor to ceiling."

Sven Watchman said that if, on the other hand, Hart-

Benoni

vigsen would lend him a few dollars on the diamond for a special reason——

"What's your reason?"

"Well, supposing Ellen and I were to get married."

"Oh, it's come to that? Where are you going to live with her?"

"We might live in the little back room when Fredrik Mensa's dead."

"Have you talked to Mack about it?"

"Yes, Ellen has talked to him. He's going to think about it."

Benoni also thought about it.

"I'll buy that diamond of yours and pay you cash on the nail," he said. "So you won't be hung up for a few dollars."

Before coming down from the roof, Sven takes a look round and says:

"There's that Attorney Arentsen off to the store again."

"You don't say so?"

"He's getting a regular customer. There won't be any good come of that."

Benoni thinks of Rosa and of the days when he was her sweetheart; he wags his head and says:

"Well, well, Rosa, your husband may be making big money, but!"

Sven Watchman won't hear any good of Attorney Arentsen; he doesn't even agree to the big money:

"I put it to you, Hartvigsen: is he making so much after all? He's got a few cases and gets a few dollars for them. But now, you see, he'll want all the dollars he can get. When his father dies he won't be able to live rent-free at the parish clerk's house any more, and then he'll have to build or rent a house. And then he's got his mother."

Benoni

On one pretext or another, Benoni kept Sven Watchman up on the roof till the Attorney came in sight again on his way back from the store.

"Is he walking steady?" asked Benoni.

"He's walking steady by reason of long practice," answered Sven Watchman.

He climbed down from the roof and set to work to clear up the soot in the kitchen. Benoni was there the whole time.

"I was just thinking of that bell-rope of Mack's," he said. "It was silver thread and velvet, wasn't it?"

"Silver thread and silk. And the handle was covered with red velvet."

"Do you think Mack would sell it?"

"Ah, that's it. Would you buy it?"

"I was thinking of getting a bell-rope," answered Benoni. "And I don't care about buying a cheap sort. Can you lie in bed and ring the bell?"

"Lie right there in bed and give it one or two tugs, just as you please. But it isn't absolutely necessary to go to bed every time you want to ring," says the gay Sven Watchman with a laugh, says the whimsical fellow for fun.

"I'll get a bell-rope like that from Bergen," says Benoni seriously. "I don't look at a dollar or two, and I may as well have a few extra things about my house." ....

Oh, but Benoni was not always so cock-sure that he could afford things; when the night was still and long, he was often filled with ugly doubts of his position. What did he possess after all? Besides the five thousand dollars which Mack, the scoundrel, had swindled him out of, he had nothing but a dwelling-house and a boat-house; the seine would soon be worthless. It was not cheerful to fall asleep with such thoughts. ...

On Sundays Benoni put on his best clothes and went

Benoni

to church. He had a hope of getting a sight of a certain person at church, and that was what made him dress up so finely every time with two jackets and a pair of seaboots whose glazed tops were beyond compare. Then one Sunday he walked home from church in an unusually dismal frame of mind. Now Arn Drier had come back from Bergen with the *Funtus* and had made Benoni's own particular trip pretty smartly and with Benoni's own luck. Soon it would be the easiest thing in the world for anybody to make the great Bergen voyage. And the *Funtus* was laden, as usual, with goods for the store, and besides there was a monstrously big and heavy case which took eight men to handle: it was the new instrument that Mack had bought. Benoni stood speechless when he heard of this instrument and of the shining new silver with which Mack had also provided himself. Where did the ruined scoundrel get the money from? And the instrument was placed in Mack's big parlour and tried by Rosa Arentsen: a few gentle touches with the tips of her fingers, and then the young wife ran off in tears, so marvellous was the tone of the new instrument.

But Benoni had another and a terrible cause for his despair: the annual assessment list was now posted for inspection and Benoni was evilly treated therein, he was no longer assessed for property.

Benoni turned pale as he stood reading this and he thought people looked at him with compassion. He laughed and said: "It's a fine thing my taxes have come down!" but it grieved him so that his lips trembled. As he walked home from church, he made up his mind to go and see the assessment commissioner and say a friendly word to him; aye, he'd laugh and give him a real good shake of the hand for letting him off property tax, ha-ha.

Aron of the Hope caught him up. Benoni frowned:

Benoni

a few months ago it was only well-to-do people who ventured to overtake Benoni Hartvigsen on the road and walk alongside him. When Aron greeted him with "Peace!" Benoni answered with "Good day!" to mark the gulf between their stations.

Aron chatted about wind and weather in the usual way before coming to the point: couldn't Hartvigsen give him a little help?

"What is it?"

It was the lawsuit. Attorney Arentsen had already got one of his cows, and the other was signed away to him. But now Aron's wife had said stop to this other cow; it should never leave the byre alive.

"I haven't any help for you," said Benoni, humiliating himself painfully. "You've seen the assessment to-day, they say I've no property at all, he-he."

"Yes, that's the queerest thing ever I heard. Which of us has any property, I'd like to know?" . . . And Aron mentioned the rocks: couldn't Hartvigsen buy the rocks off him?

"Why do you come and offer the rocks to me?"

"Who should I go to? I go to the man who can afford it. I've talked with Arentsen about these blessed rocks, he can't afford it; I've talked to Mack about them, he can't afford it."

When he heard this, Benoni said:

"I'll think about it. Have you talked to the Lightkeeper?"

"The Lightkeeper? He sent stones to the Professor in Christiania for me and got an answer that it's lead ore with silver in it. What more can the Lightkeeper do? You're the only man who can afford it."

"Ah, well," said Benoni when he had thought a hurried thought or two; "the money's all the same to me, it isn't a question of that. I'll buy the rocks."

Benoni

"You'll do me an everlasting favour."

"You can come to me to-morrow," said Benoni in Mack's curt manner, and nodded as Mack was in the habit of nodding.

Now he was in for it. . . .

Next day Benoni had another talk with Schöning the lightkeeper. The shrivelled man felt proud and happy at the smallest importance being attached to his opinion; at any rate these rocks that he had been looking at for years were going to change hands, something was going to be done about them, his idea was no longer stone-dead. The Lightkeeper advised giving a good price for that mile of rocks, ten thousand dollars was the lowest.

But Aron of the Hope and Benoni were sensible men both of them and saw well enough that the Lightkeeper was a bit above himself. Benoni, on the contrary, was himself all over and by no means inclined to buy the rocks at a fancy price: ore and silver were not in his line, but with a certain amount of labour and outlay he could split these rocks for a good stretch along the shore and the common and make a fine drying-ground for fish out of them. For it was on the cards that one day he would be buying fish from Lofoten on his own account and then he'd want the drying-ground.

He and Aron agreed upon a hundred dollars for the rocks and the scrub that grew on them. The Sheriff's officer it was who drew up the deed.

But as he laid down the pen, Benoni felt himself Aron's benefactor and guardian to such a degree that he said:

"But this money's not to go to the Attorney, you understand. You can't afford that."

"H'm. As to that . . . What, all this money? God forbid!"

"How much is your cow pawned for?"

Benoni

"Twelve dollars."

Benoni counted out twelve dollars and gave them to Aron: "That's for young Nikolai. And that's the end of your lawsuit!" Then he counted up the eighty-eight dollars, wrapped them in paper and said: "And this —this is not for young Nikolai."

Aron of the Hope knew all about the connexion between Benoni and Rosa, the Attorney's wife, so he nodded as he took the money, and said:

"This is not for young Nikolai, no."

"Well, let me see that you keep your word."

Oh, it was great to lay down the law and act the Mack and enjoy folks' respect! Now let Aron spread the tale of what Benoni Hartvigsen had said and done. . . .

The Sheriff's officer took the deed with him to send to the District Judge for registration.

XXI

BENONI could not get rid of what he called the low-spirited feeling about his head. He had seen Rosa once and only once since their last farewell on the road in the spring; how she stayed indoors! Pleasant journey to Rosa; but to think that she never went to church, was never to be seen along the road, was no longer a constant visitor at Sirilund as in the old days! And now the old parish clerk was dead, so she no longer had an invalid to look after. Oh, well, what was Rosa to him?

And in spite of Benoni's having been to see the assessment commissioner and laughed and chaffed with him, the appeal committee had not seen fit to award him taxable property. It was a conspiracy to drag him down and make him his own equal again.

Benoni went through bad days and nights. God knows, perhaps they were right and he was going downhill. All that he had done to show people his means had been done in vain: he had swept his kitchen chimney of the fat smoke of roasting, had squandered a big lump of money out of his slender balance on some drying-rocks which perhaps he would never be able to use, and then in his pride he had bought a diamond to cut glass with! Yet everybody thought Benoni was hardly solvent; one fine day Mack of Sirilund was sure to take him for debt! My yoke is grievous, thought the biblical Benoni; and in worldly language he thought something like this: I never row but what I'm backing water.

Benoni

Christmas Eve came; Benoni sat at home. It was not like last year when he was Hartvigsen and had an invitation to Mack's. Oh, but now the great Mack of Sirilund had better look out for himself! The money, the five thousand dollars, had fallen due some weeks ago, but Benoni had expressly omitted to go and claim it, simply to see whether he would get another invitation this year to Christmas Eve at Sirilund. To be sure, Benoni was not anxious to spare Mack now, it was not for his sake he was giving time; it was only that Rosa would certainly be at Mack's this Christmas Eve. . . . What then? Again, what was Rosa to him?

He began to take it out of himself in little fits of economy. He had now traded away so much of his ready money that he would soon have to ask Mack for credit at the store, a step he tried to put off as long as possible. He put the cream in his cup first and poured in the coffee after, just to save the stirring with a silver spoon. Then he sprinkled salt round the wick of the candle and said: "There, let it burn in Jesu name!" But the salt was put there to make the candle burn so thriftily, so thriftily, and last well through the evening. There he sat in his loneliness, eating the supper left out for him and drinking a couple of drams to it. When that was done he read prayers to himself and drank a little something to them too, and then he sang the hymn. But after that there was nothing more to do.

And now Rosa would be sitting in the parlour at Sirilund and playing on the new instrument. She had such velvety hands, Rosa. . . .

Benoni nodded as he sat at the table and dropped into a doze. But the candle sputtered and crackled with the salt and now and then gave a little pop which woke him up. Then he started brooding for the thousandth time over his whole existence and Rosa and his means and the heirlooms and the seine outfit. Aye, aye, so he was on the road to bankruptcy, there it was. And when he remembered the drying-rocks he had just bought of Aron of the Hope, he had the idea that these rocks would make a small show in his estate, they would swell his assets, that was all they were good for. Very well; if he was a beggar he was a beggar, he would send Rosa the spoon and fork he had once put aside for her. . . .

Then Sven Watchman knocked and came into the room.

"Well, I must say!" Benoni instantly exclaimed; "you don't mean to tell me you've eaten and drunk your Christmas dinner already? You shall have all you want here," he said, cheering up. He paid no particular attention to Sven, but went on with his chat: "I can't make out what's wrong with the candle; they're wretched candles we're getting now, they don't give any light."

"It's light enough," replied Sven Watchman absently. He seemed in a dull and gloomy frame of mind.

Benoni poured out a dram, made the other drink it and filled up again a few times. Then he arranged the table, brought out the food and chatted all the time:

"Well, you've come from a grander table than mine, but if you don't despise it——"

"I do not despise it," replied Sven, and he helped himself to a little and began to chew rather laboriously.

"It's too dry for you," said Benoni, filling his glass again. "Well, there was a big spread at Sirilund as usual?"

"There was."

"H'm. Were there any strangers?"

"I don't know, I didn't go in."

"You didn't go in?"

"No. I didn't feel like it."

Benoni

Benoni looked at him in surprise.

"No, I went and walked about a bit," he explained, "and then I thought I'd come up to you."

"You're not like yourself this evening. I reckon something's happened to you," said Benoni.

Whatever Sven Watchman drank made no difference to him, he sat there as pale and absent as when he came in. So probably he would get drunk all of a sudden and collapse, as is the way of sound and healthy people.

"No, I was just walking about," he grew more talkative. "And Ellen, she was out there too. And then little Ellen had to go in, I don't know."

"Yes, I suppose she had. Was Rosa at Sirilund?"

"Yes."

Benoni nodded to himself:

"Aye, aye, I'll have a talk with that Mack after the holidays."

"Are you going to have a talk with Mack?"

"I want my money."

"I've got to have a talk with Mack too. It can't go on any more like this," said Sven Watchman. "Fredrik Mensa won't die; but I'd rather get married and move into the little room anyway."

"If so be you can get her by fair means."

"By fair means or foul."

Benoni put more faith in little words than in big ones; he said, to change the subject:

"Then the Attorney must have been there too?"

"Yes, it was he who came after me."

"Came after you?"

"You see, I meant to stab her." . . . Sven Watchman drew the foreman's long butcher's knife out of his inside pocket and sat quite seriously looking at it and feeling the edge with his finger.

Benoni

"Have you gone stark mad!" exclaimed Benoni. "Let me have that knife."

But Sven Watchman put the knife back in his pocket and began to tell his story, to explain himself:

"Mack asked his housekeeper for bath water. Very well, said the housekeeper. Then he asked Ellen to come and be searched on Christmas Eve; no, Ellen wouldn't. You'd better just try! I said to her. That was this morning. Then towards evening Mack got hold of Ellen again and asked her to hide a fork about her at supper-time and come and be searched, and then she promised. When I heard that, I went to the foreman and said: Let me have the loan of that five-inch knife of yours. What do you want with it? he asks; it's too good for you to use. I want to shave my beard with it, I said. I got the knife, but I didn't shave myself with it, I stuck it in my pocket and went to Ellen. I asked Ellen to come out with me, but she was afraid of me and wouldn't come: I haven't time, she said. I asked her again and then she answered: All right, in God's name! and came out with me. Have you promised to go and be searched this evening? I asked. No, said she. You'd better just try! said I again, for then you'll be too free with yourself, and I won't have it! I can't make you men out, said Ellen, all the lot of you want me the whole time, I don't get any peace, I can hardly get a bit of sewing done even. I said: And what's more, it's me that's to have you, but I've never once got anything but No out of you; and over and above I'm going to clear out. All right, said she. Do you say all right? I ask, and I happen to shout a bit loud; then you don't know what I'm going to do! Ellen looked at me a second and then she ran into the house by the back door. I hung about, it was getting darker and darker, I went round the house and came to the front door; nobody there, the hall lamp was shining all by itself. When I came up to the servants' hall, they'd just got word that everybody was to come into the kitchen ready for supper. I went back to the front door and waited outside. In a little while Ellen came. I've been looking for you everywhere, said Ellen; please come in to supper. Then I hadn't the heart to go for her, she asked me so nicely. Is it settled that you're to go up to him this evening? I said. Yes, I suppose so, she answered. Can't you get out of it? I asked. Oh, no, I can't, she said. Then she came straight at me and threw her arms round me and kissed me. I could tell she had had a drop of something strong. So it's because you're afraid of my knife that you've had a drop of something strong? I said. I'm not afraid of your knife, she answered; Mack'll come as soon as I call out. I shall kill him too, I said. Then Ellen answered: Two can play at that."

Sven Watchman stopped to think; then he tossed off a couple of drams, fixed his eyes on Benoni and resumed:

"Two can play at that, she said."

"Well, I heard; what did she mean by that?"

"That's what I can't make out."

"Did you lay hands on her then?"

"I got hold of her hair; but she held me so tight round the body that I couldn't get at the knife. I hit her a couple of times and got her on her knees. Now call for him! said I. No, she said, I shan't call for him. And let me tell you that I've been up to his room this afternoon, she said, and I'm going to him again, nobody else shall go to him, she said. I stood and listened to her and I could feel myself going all queer. When I felt for the knife, Ellen had got it in her own hand. I pulled her hand to pieces and got back the knife—and then she wriggled just like a worm and got away from

Benoni

me on the ground; I hadn't hold of her any more and she ran into the hall. I made a dash after her and saw Arentsen standing at the parlour door and looking out into the hall. I pulled up short. What's all this noise? asked Arentsen, and shut the door again. Ellen held her hair in her hand and got away upstairs. I was going after her, but Arentsen put his head out of the door again and watched."

Benoni didn't understand such wild doings, he listened to the story as if it were something out of the papers. Sven Watchman mechanically emptied another glass and began to lose grip.

"So I didn't get her killed," he said.

"If all you've been telling me is true," said Benoni, "and you've been like a savage monster with her," said he, "then what I'll have to do will be to take a rope and tie you up."

"Yes, it happened all right."

"This evening?"

"Just now; this very moment."

Benoni said:

"Then I don't know that you need trouble to be sitting here in my house. You can go anywhere you like for me. Do you know how you have behaved? Like a brutish person."

Sven Watchman only sat still and thought. Then he asked:

"What can she have meant by that? That two could play at that? She's in love with him."

"With Mack?" asked Benoni in amazement.

"Yes."

Sven sat leaning forward, thinking and blinking his eyes; the stupor was growing on him. It began to dawn on Benoni that this crazy fellow was suffering keenly and at the end of his endurance. Ch, but he must have

Benoni

been quite out of his wits if he thought Ellen Parlourmaid was in love with Mack.

"Now see and sit quite still for a bit," said Benoni. "Then I don't know but what I might go with you to Sirilund. And you can feel quite safe if I'm with you."

But Sven Watchman collapsed rapidly after the excitement he had been through; presently his eyes were closed. With a great effort he opened them again and said:

"Do you think she hurt herself with the knife? Well, come on, let's go."

He tried to get up, but fell back again and could not stand. Benoni took the knife out of his pocket.

XXII

A FEW days after Christmas, Benoni went to Mack's office. Mack guessed his business at once and said:

"Good day, Hartvigsen. I was just thinking of sending for you; we have an account outstanding which I should like to settle."

Benoni was all excitement. It surely couldn't be possible that Mack was able to pay him his money?

"First I must express my regret that I could not invite you on Christmas Eve," said Mack. "It could not be managed this year."

"Oh, why talk of a thing like that!" answered Benoni rather bitterly. "I'm not of the right rank and quality!"

"Oh, aren't you? Let me tell you, my dear Hartvigsen, that there is nobody I would rather see here than you. But out of consideration for yourself and others, I had to leave you out."

"I shouldn't have bitten her," said Benoni.

"H'm. I am sure you will understand how unpleasant it would have been for—well, for everybody. The husband was also present, you see."

Benoni had a suspicion that Mack had done right, and gave in:

"All right. I didn't mean it."

Mack opened his desk and lifted his cash-box by the handle. It seemed gloriously heavy in his thin hand. Suddenly he checked himself and said:

"There's one thing: can you take the *Funtus* to Lofoten this year?"

Benoni

"Can I . . . the *Funtus?*"

"As you did last year."

"Isn't Arn Drier to have the schooner?"

"No," replied Mack curtly.

Pause.

"You understand, don't you, that Arn Drier is very well to send to Bergen," said Mack; "it is an easy matter to deliver a cargo. But I can't send him to *buy* cargo for three vessels. That requires brains."

"But if he was good enough for the Bergen trip . . ." Benoni began.

"And above all," Mack went on, "it requires responsibility. Arn Drier isn't worth a penny, but you I can trust with as many thousands as I please. You are equal to it."

It did Benoni a power of good to here these words from Mack's lips after all the gossip of bankruptcy he had had to put up with. He answered:

"It isn't everybody that thinks that. They don't give me any property in the assessment this time."

"Lucky man! No property, no income, no taxes. . . . And Villads the wharfinger and Man Ole are to sail the sloops, as last year. So no doubt you'll take Sven Watchman with you in the *Funtus*."

His ingrained respect for Mack of Sirilund, his innate, instinctive obedience to this master of all around, forbade Benoni's declining the proposal off-hand; moreover, he knew that the man who could restore public belief in his fortune was this same Mack. He said:

"If I durst call myself the man for the job."

"You were good enough for it last year."

Then said Benoni:

"But let that be, it isn't the money."

"The money?" asked Mack in surprise. "Here's the money," he said, laying his hand flat on the cash-box.

Benoni

"Ah, that's it."

"But the fact is, I have use for the money," said Mack, coming straight to the point. "I should like an extension of time; I want to buy fish with it. I have a proposal to make: you go to Lofoten yourself and buy cargo for the three vessels, buy what fish you please. In the autumn, when I sell, you'll get your money with interest."

"No," replied Benoni, "I've made up my mind . . . No, certainly not. . . . And what security have I that I'll get my money in the autumn?"

"You have a lien on the fish, haven't you?" replied Mack, surprised again.

"Oh, then I have a lien on the fish?"

"Naturally. The fish is yours till I sell it. Then the money's yours."

Benoni began to connect this new project with the drying-ground he had bought; now he would have use for his rocks, for now he would have fish. With rather shaky reasoning he remarked:

"But if I buy fish with my own money, it isn't really you that I'm buying fish for."

"My dear Hartvigsen, to buy fish you need vessels; I have three, you haven't one. In the next place, I'm trying to help you now as before: you must begin to get your hand in. For I suppose it is your intention one day to buy fish for your own account; what else do you want with the drying-ground you have gone in for? Very well, relying on your brains and your luck, I give you a chance this year to get your hand in on my account: if I make a little, so much the better; if I lose, the loss is mine and not yours. You simply draw your interest on the money, besides your wages."

Benoni stood and thought a long while; then he said:

"Anyhow, I'd have liked to have a sight of the money."

Mack opened the cash-box and took out bundle after

bundle of notes. And Benoni's eyebrows went up in surprise till the folds of his low forehead met his shock of hair.

"Do you want to count them?" asked Mack.

"No, I only wanted . . . No, not at all . . ."

Benoni left Mack's office just as penniless as he had entered it. At the last moment he had managed to remember to apply for credit at the store for the time being, till the autumn, when the dried fish was sold. And Mack didn't say No, far from it; he allowed Benoni credit at the store. "We'll manage that," said Mack. And though Benoni had a mortal horror of the cross-tempered store clerk Steen, he couldn't avoid going to him.

"If I send my servant for a thing or two from the store, you'll have to put it down," said Benoni.

"Has Mack promised you credit?" asked Steen the store clerk.

Benoni swallowed all the insolence of this and answered with a smile:

"Yes. I suppose he thought I was safe for it. What do you think?"

"I? It's all the same to me who I put things down for. They're all in our books, every one of them."

"Ha-ha. Why don't you say *my* books?"

Benoni meant to have a try at dressing down this counter-jumping squirt to his natural size, he had got far too uppish and insolent. And—what do you think!—now Rosa and the Attorney had adopted one of Steen's children, a little girl of six, and made use of her to run errands for them and to chat with; but since then Steen the store clerk had grown prouder than ever, because his little girl had got a new dress. "That's folks!" said he to Benoni; "they dress up the child like a princess and she gets more to eat than she wants." "I reckon it's because the Attorney can't get a child himself," said Sven Watchman, who was listening. They wrangled about this for awhile; Sven Watchman asserted that the Attorney's glory would be short-lived; now he had had to give up the parish clerk's house and take lodgings at the blacksmith's: was that a house and home for a fine lady? And what kind of a husband was it Rosa of the parsonage had got? The man spent his time drinking here at the spirit counter. For shame! "If I was watchman here," said Sven, "I'd just lay my hand on his shoulder and say: You come along with me!"

Benoni took Sven Watchman outside and said:

"We're to go to Lofoten again with the *Funtus*. How do you like that?"

How did Sven Watchman like it? Well, he was not keen on the trip. He had patched things up with Ellen after the mad fit of Christmas Eve; since then things had been even better between them, the knife and the beating had actually taken effect with little Ellen and reformed her. She had only clung close to him and said reproachfully: "But you're never going to do it any more, are you?" "Not much," he replied, shamefaced and uncomfortable; "and it was only that I got so hasty." But Mack himself said straight out to Ellen: "Sven Watchman will have to marry you in the spring; I won't have any murders about the place."

So there stood Sven face to face with his old skipper, with no great relish for the Lofoten trip.

But now it was like this, he was buying his own fish this year, Benoni told him.

What? That was another affair. His own fish? Then Sven Watchman would join him, it would be a shame if he didn't. . . .

Benoni sailed for Lofoten in his schooner, and the two sloops went with her. So the bay lay empty of craft. And winter shrouded the whole country in snow and stillness. . . .

Meanwhile the Attorney and his wife had moved over to the blacksmith's cottage. "It's only for the time being," said Young Arentsen; "we can build later on!" They had with them the old parish clerk's widow and their adopted child, Steen the store clerk's daughter.

They were allowed to arrange the rooms as they pleased, the blacksmith kept no more than a bedroom for himself; there was tremendous washing and scrubbing, till at last the place was clean upstairs and down, and curtains were hung before some of the windows. Never had the blacksmith's house looked so nice; but then it had never been intended for gentlefolks. Rosa had a big spring-cleaning before she moved in, she was at it for several days. And a settee and the two best chairs were put in Nikolai's office for the benefit of callers; it left the parlour pretty empty and desolate, but that did not matter so much. In a few years perhaps they could afford a piano in that gaping corner towards the sea.

The Attorney put up his brass plate on the first door in the passage, and through that door he occasionally passed in pursuit of his vocation and so as at any rate to use the door once a day. But nevermore did anyone appear in his office. No, it was winter, all disputes and litigation slept. Oh, why hadn't he applied for the post of fishery magistrate, as he had thought of doing? Now he was hanging about, getting more dull and vacant day by day and reduced at times to an innocent game of cribbage with the blacksmith.

Nor did the shameful way in which the Courts were treating him tend to revive the Attorney's spirits. The case of Levion of Torpelvik and Hugh Trevelyan had now been decided by the Appeal Court and lost again: the judgment of the lower court was upheld. What

Benoni

in the evening and there was no sweetness in him: the dinner was cold; his mother, the old widow, scuttled out of his way, haggard and alarmed, and Rosa began by laughing at his drunken and tousled appearance, but when he took offence at this she obstinately held her tongue and said never a word.

"You're a great comfort to me, Rosa, when I'm plunged in despair," said he.

Silence.

"The loss of this case to-day," he went on, "means, of course, that the Courts intend to ruin my business; what do you say to that?"

At last she answered:

"I don't think you ought to send the child to Sirilund for bottles."

"H'm. So that's *your* first thought when your lawyer husband loses a case!"

Silence.

"Bottles? What do you mean by that? I who can polish off two bottles and be none the worse for it; and yet I only take a few quarterns. Do you mean to say I'm a drinker?"

"No," she said. "Well, you're often at Sirilund."

"What of it? Do you want me to drop dead with boredom? No, you just hold your tongue, little Rosa. When I'm in despair I take myself out of the house, that's all."

"Then you've been more or less in despair every single day for eight months," she said.

"Yes," he answered, nodding twice to himself; "that's not altogether untrue."

To ward off further unpleasantness, she asked:

"But don't you think it would be better for Martha to go back to her mother?"

"Why so? Well, perhaps. No, certainly not. If she

does these messages of mine to the store, it gives her a chance of meeting her father. It's a very good arrangement."

Pause.

"Perhaps you ought to have taken Post Benoni after all," he said musingly.

"Do you think so?"

"Well, what do you think? I'm not the husband for you."

She looked at him. His perfectly bare crown and its contrast with the thick short hair at the back of his neck gave that neck a look of monstrous deformity. He had a sort of gnome-like air with this misshapen head, especially at this moment, when it had collapsed into his shoulders.

As she made no answer, he said again:

"No, I never thought you would turn out such a tiresome girl."

"Then perhaps you had better say that I am no wife for you."

Young Arentsen sat looking at his hands, then he raised his eyes to the wall and said:

"Well, well, you can say what you like, Rosa; there's no love but stolen love."

At that a sudden change came over her face and the light faded slowly from her eyes, like a setting sun.

"From the moment love acquires legality it becomes hoggish," Young Arentsen concluded. "And from that moment it becomes a habit. But at the same moment *love* has evaporated."

are coming back from Lofoten and Nikolai ought to be at home so that people can find him. How is he to get on otherwise? Just think, standing here at the bar, a lawyer!"

"Exaggerations. No, but, what's worse, he's losing his cases."

"Yes, he's losing his cases too."

"You ought to have taken Benoni," said Mack.

"Benoni? Certainly not," she replied hotly, turning red. "And you know that quite well. I ought to have taken the man I took."

"You did an uncommonly silly thing. You went dead against my advice."

Rosa broke off:

"So I may ask Steen for a few little things to go on with?" . . .

There came Benoni, walking along the road to Sirilund, and he met Rosa and little Martha coming from the store. When he saw who it was, he gave a start and slackened his pace. Well, he had no reason to be afraid of Rosa, besides, there was no possibility of getting away in the middle of the bare road. But after all this time and all that had happened, it took some doing to keep right ahead. There—now she in her turn had caught sight of what was in front of her, and her steps began to waver. She looked as if she might sink into the ground.

"Good day," he said. He saw at a glance how these last months had changed her. Little Martha curtsied; it was a charming sight, but had an unfamiliar look to Benoni; it was only gentlefolk's children who curtsied. And this child's curtsy at once reminded him—they are gentlefolks these, Rosa has become a lady since we met.

"Good day, and welcome home from Lofoten," Rosa answered, as was right and proper.

Benoni

"Can you carry that heavy pail?" Benoni asked the child.

Oh, goodness knows what he said! It was a good thing he had the child to help him out. And Rosa too bent down in her confusion and asked little Martha:

"Yes, isn't it too heavy for you? Wouldn't you like me to carry it?"

"No."

"Then you can carry this parcel instead."

"Oh, but the parcel's not so heavy," answered Martha in displeasure.

"It's not so heavy as the pail, no," laughed Benoni. "And that must be very heavy. . . . Isn't that Steen the store clerk's little girl?"

"Yes."

After this introduction Benoni got over the worst of his embarrassment and said:

"Yes, it's many a day since I saw you."

"Oh, yes, time flies."

"You haven't changed a bit," he said from pure kindness.

"Oh, well, it isn't *so* long since we met."

"It will soon be just a year. In a week's time. And you're quite well?"

"Yes, thanks."

"Aye, aye, well, well. It's a great change. Married and all. And now you're a fine lady."

"The pail's full of treacle," said Martha.

Benoni only looked at the child and didn't hear. But Rosa was a little ashamed of the humble sweetstuff she had been buying at the store and said:

"Yes, that's for you. You're so fond of it, you know. . . . Children and treacle!" she said, looking up at Benoni.

"Ah, children and treacle!" he said in turn. . . . Now

Benoni

Benoni still took treacle and lots of it on his bread and butter and thought it good; but Rosa, it seemed, didn't take it, so hers was a fine house. . . . "Well, well, you want to get home," he said; "don't let me keep you."

"You're not keeping me," she answered. "Now, Martha, we're going to walk a little farther. . . . There's one thing I wanted to say to you: I want to beg your pardon for not sending back—you know what. It's too bad of me."

The ring and the cross once more!

"You needn't trouble to talk about that," he said.

"I have thought of it so often, but——"

"If it makes you uneasy, just sling it into the sea. Then it'll be out of sight as well as out of mind—as the saying is."

She remembered that she had already disposed of the ring and given it to a corpse; oh, but she couldn't enter into a long explanation about that.

"That you should think I would sling it into the sea!" she said.

"Well, won't you?"

"No."

A little warm current of joy ran through him, he was so grateful that he could not help saying:

"I have one or two other things that were meant for you; but perhaps I can't send them?"

"No, you mustn't," she replied, shaking her head.

"No, no. It was only a miserable little spoon and fork. Well, of course, they're silver, but still . . . It's only a wretched sort of silver, you see. For that matter, you could have the full dozen if you liked."

"Many thanks, but . . ."

"Oh, no, it's not a thing to offer you. It was only just an idea. . . . Well, I'm keeping you here," he said again abruptly, making to go. He was as nervous as a

Benoni

boy at the thought that he had gone too far with his talk about the silver.

She seized the opportunity, nodded and said:

"Well, good-bye."

"Good-bye," he answered. He was strangely flustered; he made a little attempt at offering his hand, but, on seeing no reciprocal movement, he took hold of Martha's pail in his confusion and lifted it."

"Oh, what a heavy pail! You must have a penny for being such a strong little girl," he said, and he gave her a silver coin. Not a bad idea, he thought, it got him over the worst. For that matter, he was not clearly conscious of anything.

And Martha forgot to curtsy and thank him. When she was reminded of it, the big strange man had gone. Rosa said: "Run after him," and Martha put down the pail and ran, curtsied and thanked him and came back. Benoni stood smiling and watched her.

Benoni slowly went on his way. He had not been in such a state of emotion for a year. He stared before him, thinking; at times he forgot to walk and stood still for a moment. And her I once held in my arms, her that's going along there. Ah, well, Rosa, it can't have been ordained any other way. . . . What kind of clothes was she wearing? A cloak? Yes, perhaps it was a cloak. He had seen nothing.

He entered Mack's office, reported his return from Lofoten and produced his accounts. He was still in his meek and mild mood, and, face to face with Mack, he dropped saying my fish and my cargo—as he had meant to do—and merely inquired whether his employer was satisfied and whether he would begin washing the fish tomorrow. And he supposed Arn Drier was the one who would have charge of the drying as before?

"Of course," answered Mack. "It's his job."

Benoni

Benoni had had a kind of idea that he himself would superintend the drying of his own fish. What else was he to do this summer? But now Mack had put a stopper on that. And Benoni was not in the mood to start another wrangle with Mack just after his wonderful adventure on the road.

Mack clearly intended to put him back at a distance. He said not a word about the fish being Benoni's property pure and simple; on the other hand, he raised questions about one or two items of the accounts:

"Why did you buy all that fish on Monday the 13th at such a high price? On that day fish was quoted at fivepence less per hundred." . . . And Mack produced an express message to prove it. Oh, that great man Mack, he had an eye to everything!

Benoni said:

"It was this way, you see, two weeks later I got fish a whole sixpence cheaper than any other buyer. I suppose you had an express about that too? It was a bargain."

"Who with?"

"With some of the men from here who wanted to make a trip home. They were short of a bit of money. But I got it back with interest after Easter."

"Supposing those boats had been lost on the trip home?"

"I had to risk that," replied Benoni. "You'd have done the same for them yourself in my place."

"But *you* had no business to do it."

Benoni answered with irritation:

"Just as much as you, I reckon."

Mack shrugged his shoulders. He didn't invite Benoni into his parlour for a drink either, but ended the interview by opening the door of the store. When they had passed through, Mack with his own hand poured out a big glass of cognac for Benoni and offered it to him.

Benoni

Here? At the spirit counter? Mack of Sirilund must have forgotten his man! In that place Benoni himself could buy a dram and pay for it. He was offended and said:

"No, thanks."

Mack gave a surprised laugh:

"Here I pour you out a glass and you refuse to drink it!"

"No, thanks," said Benoni again.

Mack changed his tone and said with the same assurance:

"Ah, if they were all as sober as you, Hartvigsen! Have you brought Sven Watchman back with you? I suppose he'll be starting his drunken pranks again."

"That depends on how he's treated. Sven Watchman never touches a drop."

"We'll see that Ellen treats him properly. They're to be married now," said Mack. . . .

The days went by, one after another, but Sven and Ellen were not married. No, it was springtime now, there was strong stuff in Mack's eyes, high explosive, and he got Ellen to put off and put off her wedding. I can't spare you in the house till after the Sessions," said Mack; "and the new maid must come first," he said; "we can't be left without help." . . . The new parlour-maid who was coming was a big fine girl for her age, but she was only sixteen. And she was the second daughter of Marelius of Torpelvik and sister to Edvarda who had learnt to *speaka Englisk*. Those new clothes Edvarda could afford gave her sister no peace, so she wanted to go out into service.

The Sessions came unusually early this year; the magistrates travelled in lined boots and furs. It was like the proper Sessions of old times with the District Judge himself on the bench and the Governor presiding. Folks

Benoni

could again ask their District Judge about a point of law and save attorney's fees; and in fact Attorney Arentsen's table was poorly furnished with papers and briefs compared with last year. What was there to be said? People were beginning to find that it cost money to go to law. Nobody had gained anything by it, they had all had worries and losses. Ah, Nikolai Arentsen had brought more harm than good to the place, folks said in their hearts.

Nikolai Arentsen was no longer the Law and ♂, far from it. In these last weeks since the fishermen came back from Lofoten, he had found out what it meant to fall in popular favour. He had begun last year by charging a dollar for a little piece of advice; this year he did it for half, and if a man haggled even at half a dollar he answered: "I can't do it cheaper if I'm to make a living!" But Attorney Arentsen was to descend even lower; he looked up important questions in the law-books for a couple of shillings and wrote them out laboriously on paper for sixpence extra. And yet—and yet his business did not increase; no, it went the other way.

The truth was that people had lost their faith in Attorney Arentsen, the Law. If you brought your business to him and got his opinion of a case, you generally went on to the Sheriff to find out whether this opinion was right. It was no longer a secret that Arentsen lost case after case, and not only that, but he had been fined by the great Appeal Court at Trondhjem.

So what was the use of Nikolai Arentsen attending to his business and keeping his regular hours at the office? People had deserted him. When he began shirking his office hours, his answer to his wife was: "I sat on my chair nicely and prettily and waited a whole week; nobody came. I sat there like a beauty, I nearly went mad with irresistibility; but nobody came."

People let their "cases" drop. Opponents took the op-

Benoni

portunity, when they met each other at Sirilund, to make friends again at Mack's spirit counter. "Now what I say is," one of them would begin, "that you and I have been neighbours for forty years." "Yes,—" the other would answer, "and so were our fathers before us." And when they had made a beginning their feelings got the better of them and their eyes glistened and they stood each other drinks and tried to outbid each other in neighbourly spirit. But Attorney Arentsen, he might be standing at the same counter taking a few innocent quarterns and be forced to listen to these idiotic reconciliations which took the bread out of his mouth.

There sits Attorney Arentsen in the court-room, good and drunk, pretending to be busy at his table. When he allows himself a respite and looks up from his papers and briefs, he meets the irresolute eyes of Levion of Torpelvik outside the bar. When the Appeal Court had decided his case Arentsen said: "We can take it to the Supreme Court, but then there will be preliminary expenses for counsel." Levion had left to think it over. Now he stood there from the opening of the Sessions pondering the question, till it was torture to Attorney Arentsen to meet his wild eyes. Arentsen pretended he had suddenly remembered something, and pulled out his note-book and began to turn it over. Then, as the Court adjourned, Levion of Torpelvik went straight up to the Judge with the Appeal Court judgment in his hand and wanted to know if he ought to take it further.

The District Judge seemed to have got over his attack of insomnia and religious scruples; that was only last year, when a certain deed was to be registered and a half-barrel of cloudberries had arrived by the mail-boat. Now the Judge was plump and well again and could spare the time as before for a worldly chat with folks.

Benoni

Disregarding Attorney Arentsen and the assembled public, the Judge answered:

"Whether you shall take it further, Levion? No, that you shan't. On the contrary, you and your attorney had better agree to pitch the case into your own stream. That's the opinion of the Appeal Court and myself." . . .

On the last day of the Sessions, Benoni's title-deed to the drying-rocks was read out and registered. There were not many present to hear it, but a smile appeared on every face at this new document of Benoni's. So last year he had bought a mile of bare rocks and now he was actually paying for the registry of the title-deed. That Benoni was well on the road to ruin, poor fellow.

But nobody was in near such a bad way as Attorney Arentsen. According to his promise, Mack had got him on the quiet and talked to him, but it was no use. Mack had then forbidden his assistants to sell Young Arentsen strong drink at the spirit counter; that was no use either. Young Arentsen instantly provided himself with go-betweens. On the last day of the Sessions he had mixed with men from the outlying stations and tried to barter away a new gold ring, in which he was successful. It was the ring Benoni gave Rosa.

XXIV

AT last Sven Watchman and Ellen Parlour-maid had got married. They lived in the same little room where Frederick Mensa lay and wouldn't die. And Ellen was really fond of her boy; more than once she wished aloud, oh, if she could only be done with service! But then she had to help the new maid for a while yet. And every time she had to go across to the main building, she hugged her husband with great fidelity.

Then came the time when people started hacking and hewing wood on the common again. Benoni left his cottage and strolled across to where the wood-cutters were making havoc, just to see that they didn't overstep his new boundary and cut the brushwood that grew on his rocks. He was not sorry for the chance of showing himself the owner of such a wide stretch.

But the men were only felling big timber and they knew perfectly well that they were not going to waste time on Benoni's bushes. He got no chance of playing the master and saying: "Here runs the boundary, all the wood on this side is mine!" The men just looked up, saw it was only Benoni, and turned back to their work. Oh, how he could feel them jeering at him for buying these rocks!

That hushed him and he went meekly about from group to group, saying:

"Bless the work!"

"Thanks, it wants some blessing. There'll soon be no wood left on the common."

They talked about this for a while. Benoni threw out

Benoni

a hint that he wanted hands for clearing his drying-ground; now was the time.

But nobody was ready to take it on. They seemed nervous about their wages with such a poverty-stricken man.

"What did he want with a drying-ground?" they asked.

Benoni answered that he intended to buy a cargo of fish next winter.

Nobody believed that. Why, he had no vessels to carry it.

"I shall have to buy myself a little sloop," said Benoni.

Then they laughed among themselves at the idea of Benoni buying a sloop.

And nobody called him Hartvigsen.

As he was standing there, two strangers in check suits came across the common; it was Sir Hugh Trevelyan again and another swell with him. They had a local man to carry their traps.

Benoni gave them a greeting and all the men round about did the same; but the two Britons made no response. They just walked on, saying a word or two to each other and knocking chips off the rocks; Sir Hugh's eyes were stiff with drink. In a minute or two the group had passed.

"Now Marelius of Torpelvik will get some more money for his salmon," said the wood-cutters.

"And his daughter Edvarda a father for her child."

"Aye, aye, there'll be a bit of money knocking about. Ah, that Marelius was lucky to have the girl."

As Benoni turned to go home again, some of them called after him: "All right, Benoni, if we can draw our wages from Mack, we'll clear your rocks."

"Wages?" said Benoni, deeply hurt. "So you think Mack of Sirilund's better than me? Let me tell you I have five thousand dollars with that same Mack."

Benoni

"Ah, you'll never see them again," was the answer.

And yet Mack enjoyed everybody's confidence and Benoni nobody's. . . .

One day a message came to Benoni that Sir Hugh Trevelyan wanted to speak to him. And it was Marelius of Torpelvik who brought the message.

"What does he want with me?" asked Benoni.

"I don't know."

"Tell him that Benoni Hartvigsen is to be found here at his residence."

Marelius tried to raise objections, but Benoni replied:

"Ask him if he'd send a message like that to Mack of Sirilund. He can make up his mind I don't count myself any cheaper."

Benoni happened that very day to have been wildly annoyed by that wretched Steen the store clerk reminding him of what he owed for groceries.

"What then?" asked Benoni. "Doesn't Mack owe me five thousand dollars?"

"I don't know anything about that," replied Steen. "But at any rate it's another account. Your servant has been here getting goods all winter and spring; it mounts up to a good sum now."

"What the hell's it got to do with you?" asked Benoni furiously. "You puppy, that's what you are. And you skinny will-o'-the-wisp, that's what you are. It would serve you right if I took and let down your breeches and gave you a hiding."

Steen the store clerk did not venture to carry it further, he muttered tamely:

"I only tell you, I just mention it for regularity's sake. I put down anything that I'm asked to, it's all the same to me who it goes down to. But it's Mack that'll suffer for it."

"Has Mack been talking to you about my store debts?

Benoni

Then he'd have done better to have held his tongue. For that fish drying out on the rocks yonder isn't Mack's fish, it's my fish."

"You'd better talk to Mack himself about all this," said Steen, and fetched Mack from the office.

Benoni grew quieter at once and said nothing more about the fish.

"Do you wish to speak to me?" asked Mack.

"No, it's Steen here that . . . Well, it's about my store debts, they can stand over till autumn, can't they?"

"Yes," answered Mack; "I don't press you," he said.

Benoni turned to Steen the store clerk in triumph:

"There, you hear that!"

"I only mentioned it by the way," said Steen. "It was nothing to get so wild about."

"Was there anything else?" asked Mack.

"No. H'm. Not that I know of."

Mack, the proud magnate, had no desire to be mixed up in his assistant's arguments with the customers; he turned and went back to the office. . . .

A week later Benoni was down in his boat-house by himself, seeing to the seine and the boats. He was condemned to inactivity. He had worked hard the whole week trying to collect a crew for another trip with the seine; but the good neighbours no longer had faith in his luck and would not go out. Only Sven Watchman had at once got Mack's permission to go for one. It was summer now, the only wood required in the whole of Sirilund was for the kitchen, and Sven wanted to go in spite of being newly married—well, perhaps because he was married.

Benoni was standing at the door of the boat-house, looking across at the drying-ground, which was swarming with men under the command of Arn Drier. Couldn't he muster a crew for his seine among all those sixty

Benoni

hands? The days had been fine and warm lately, the fish must soon be ready for stowing on board. Benoni shut the boat-house door and walked along the rocks; there could be no harm in taking a look at his own fish for once.

The weather was calm and warm, the gulls shone in the sunlight, looking like flocks of silver scissors gently working through the air.

Benoni was afraid of offending Arn Drier with his visit, so he went about it gingerly and said: "Bless the work! Seems to be getting on fine."

"Nothing to complain of," replied Arn, and found something to do.

Benoni took up a fish, dropped it, took up another, weighed fish after fish in his hand; there couldn't possibly be any offence in that. Then he said:

"It feels pretty near dry. What do you think?"

"What I think? Well, you know a lot more about it than I do," muttered Arn, moving off.

Benoni then made free to go around and examine his own fish. He straightened out the crushed dorsal fins and looked to see if the folds were dry; he treated the pectoral fins in the same way, though that was not so important; finally he bent the whole fish double to feel if there was spring in it. "A few more dry days and this will be a fine lot to ship," said he. No answer from the men. Benoni came to his real business and brought up the question of the seining; who would join him? Not a man said Yes. There stood Benoni Hartvigsen, hat in hand, among all these people, and he met with nothing but refusals. "We'd rather earn a little safe money here on the drying-rocks than go out seining," they said. "As far as that goes, the fish will soon be dry and you won't earn any more," Benoni objected. "Well, of course you know a lot more about it than Arn Drier," said they.

Benoni

A great visit was in store for Benoni on his return: the two Englishmen in checks and two men besides stood waiting for him. Marelius of Torpelvik was the spokesman and announced that Sir Hugh and the other Englishman had come on business.

"What do these folks want with me?" asked Benoni.

This time Marelius knew a little more about it: Sir Hugh had brought this gentleman out from England this year, he was a mining expert; they had spent several days prospecting among Benoni's rocks and had surveyed them; perhaps they would buy some of them.

Benoni thought it was a trifling question of shore rights, a few dollars, and said:

"Ah, we'll see if that Benoni and I will sell."

"Won't you sell them?"

"No. I'm not so put to it as that."

Instead of being silenced or knocked flat by Benoni's words, Marelius found a stone and sat down on it.

"It might be that Sir Hugh would give a pot of money for those rocks," he said.

"What then?"

They took a long time beating about the bush; Benoni was continually on his guard against anybody supposing he was forced to sell a few fathoms of shore rights. Meanwhile the two Englishmen stood apart and behaved as if Benoni did not exist; they chatted together very quietly and pointed now and then to the plans. But though Sir Hugh was extremely drunk and stiff about the eyes, the mining expert treated him with great respect, so the same Sir Hugh must have been a mighty man. He pretended he didn't understand anybody's Norwegian but Marelius', so everything had to go through him. Humble as a slave, Marelius went up and reported that Benoni would not sell.

Yes, it was just as though a really smart angel stood

Benoni

by Benoni's side and prompted him. His blunt refusals had their effect on the Englishman. Obstinate to the point of invincibility, Sir Hugh had got it into his head that he and nobody else had discovered these rich rocks on a fishing trip to Nordland in Norway, and now he was going to buy them. Therefore he had brought a mining expert to prospect. The rocks had changed ownership since last year, when perhaps Aron of Hope would have let them go for a trifle; but probably that made no great difference when it came to the point; Benoni would be sure to sell. And Sir Hugh wanted to buy the rocks for a little boy that the girl Edvarda had presented him with while he was away. Ah, that little boy, a marvel, a regular miracle! Sir Hugh measured him and weighed him; drunken and hysterical, the happy father went about proclaiming the child's loveliness. There was *Sir* and *Hon.* on his letters, but that was nothing to being father of this marvel. "You hold him all the time," he said to the mother; "can't you let me hold him a little?" In his eccentricity Sir Hugh connected the child with the mines which he and nobody else had discovered, and he meant to transfer these riches to his son. He confided this to the mining expert. "What a rich man my son will be some day!" he said; "I shall come over every year to see him getting richer and richer; the rocks will just stay there going up in value!" The mining expert treated the affair more soberly; the specimens he had assayed were very promising; but he must make a proper round of the whole big field.

And now the round had been made; the mining expert was no longer in doubt that they were face to face with a very rich property. . . .

Finally Marelius asked in Sir Hugh's name how much Benoni wanted for the rocks.

"I'm buying fish next winter and shall have use for

Benoni

my rocks," said Benoni. "But if he only wants a few fathoms of shore rights, he can have them for nothing. I'm not such a curmudgeon as all that."

"But Sir Hugh wants to buy all the rocks, the whole mile of them."

"Oh! What will he give for it?"

"Five thousand dollars," said Marelius.

Benoni felt a ripple of astonishment go through him; he looked from one to the other and finally asked Sir Hugh himself if that was his bid.

Sir Hugh nodded. Beyond that he didn't seem willing to have any dealings with so irrelevant a person as Benoni; Sir Hugh turned away from him.

Benoni, that smart lad of old days, guessed at once that business was meant. So after all the Professor in Christiania was right and there was galena and silver in great quantities. Five thousand dollars.

"I'll think about it," said Benoni.

"What'll you think about?" Marelius took it upon himself to ask.

Benoni was equal to his bounce:

"Never you mind, Marelius. I've got a writing from the Professor in Christiania for what there is in my rocks."

"What's that about a Professor in Christiania?" cried Sir Hugh all of a sudden, pale with resentment. "It is *I* who discovered the rocks." ... He looked Benoni up and down from the corner of his eye.

"Oh, all right," Benoni gave in; "I dare say you did. I'm not going to dispute about that. But the rocks, they're mine."

Benoni was given time to think it over till the next mail-boat was in. And then the attorney from town would be on board.

XXV

BENONI passed the following days in a state of extraordinary excitement. He shrank from confiding in anybody; perhaps when the Englishman had slept off his drink he wouldn't come back at all, and then Benoni would be left the laughing-stock of the whole place. But as the time drew near for the mail-boat's arrival, Benoni could not hold out any longer, and he strolled across to Sirilund to get hold of Sven Watchman. The two shipmates retired to a secluded spot and Benoni insisted on dead silence before disclosing his secret.

Sven Watchman stood for a long time pondering over it.

"All this is very fine," he said with some emotion. "Five thousand dollars!"

"But what is your opinion about it?"

"My opinion? H'm. I was just thinking it over."

"Do you believe the Englishman will come back?"

"Just as soon as the mail-boat's in, he'll come," answered Sven with decision. "Do you think a man like that, a prince I might call him—— They're made of money, these Englishmen. When I arrested an English sailor in town, he paid up what was asked and thought nothing of it."

"What sort of a figure do you think I should put the rocks at?"

Sven Watchman thought it over:

"If there's to be any sense in it, you must ask ten thousand for those rocks."

Benoni

"Oh, you think that?"

"That's my firm conviction. Isn't there silver in them? ... Look here," said Sven suddenly, "you must ask the Lightkeeper."

Benoni shook his head:

"No, I'm not going to tell anybody but you."

"But do you know what, Hartvigsen? if there's to be a lawyer on one side, there'll have to be one on the other. You ought to go and get Arentsen."

Again Benoni bluntly refused. . . .

The mail-boat was in, the lawyer from town had come. He took up his quarters at Sirilund, as he always did at Sessions time. Next day he came and wanted to get Benoni to go with him to visit Sir Hugh. But Benoni refused. His real reason was that he had made up his mind after all to speak to the Lightkeeper that day; but he gave the lawyer to understand that he was not so almighty keen on the whole business. When the lawyer had started on his walk across the common, Benoni betook himself to Lightkeeper Schöning.

"About those rocks," he began straight away; "do you think I ought to sell them again?"

"No," said the Lightkeeper; "they're too good for that."

"I'm offered five thousand dollars for them."

"Eh?"

"By a rich Englishman."

Oh, that Paul Schöning, keeper of a lighthouse of the fourth class, withered to the roots, petrified in self-contempt and cynicism, what was happening to him now? He was appointed guardian and director of this light: he lighted it and let its iron head scatter sheer stupidity fourteen miles to seaward, he extinguished it and it stood there in contrasted vacancy inside and out; it was so game, so game, all empty-handed as it was, standing up to the sea, as it were, in carpet slippers.

Benoni

Lightkeeper Schöning felt a change take place within him at Benoni's words, something changed places with something else. The rocks, his own idea, the idea he had cherished for many years, were again in motion and acquired a new owner, an Englishman, a prince. So, after all, Paul Schöning's brains were not the most despicable in the whole world!

"Ah," he said, leaning forward in his chair to conceal his excitement. "H'm. Five thousand. But I hope to God in heaven you'll refuse that offer."

The unwonted solemnity of the Lightkeeper's words made Benoni prick up his ears.

"I see," he said; "then perhaps I ought to ask a little more?"

"I said ten thousand the first time," the Lightkeeper went on; "now I'd say a million."

"No, be serious, man."

The Lightkeeper thought it over; he actually took up a pencil as though to reckon it out, and said:

"A million. That's the nearest I can make it."

Benoni was far too busy to sit here and enjoy one of Lightkeeper Schöning's usual crazy yarns. He got up and said:

"So you think I can ask something like ten thousand?"

The Lightkeeper also rose to his feet, and at that moment he inspired Benoni with some of his own fantastic belief in the wealth of the rocks.

"If it was the last word I was ever to utter, you shan't sell them under a million," he said.

This visit only served to increase Benoni's perplexity; he just looked in at home for a snack of food and then went off to the Sheriff's. It was late in the evening when he reached his house again, having secured the assistance of the Sheriff's officer for the next day.

In the morning he put on his best clothes and kept run-

Benoni

ning in and out of doors from sheer restlessness. He drifted down to the boat-house, where he stopped in the middle of the mud floor, looked around and went out again. All at once he made up his mind to carry out the idea which had matured in him during the night: he would have to go to Nikolai Arentsen after all. The time was eleven in the forenoon.

Benoni came to the blacksmith's cottage, read Arentsen's name on the door of the office and knocked. No answer. He looked in; nobody there. Then he heard somebody splashing water and scrubbing a floor farther in; he went on and knocked. No answer. He opened the door and entered the room.

It was Rosa who was scrubbing. There she was with bare arms and skirts tucked up; a short red petticoat came half-way down her calves. She hurriedly let down the skirt of her dress, showing a good deal of embarrassment beside being out of breath with her work.

"Peace!" was Benoni's greeting. "Don't take it amiss if I come in so sudden-like."

She pushed a kitchen chair forward without lifting it and imitated Benoni's local way of speaking:

"Please see and sit you down. You've come to a fine house, I must say. Here I am like a charwoman . . ." She struggled to get her sleeves over her wet elbows and walked about the room as she did so.

"Don't say a word, who cares for the like of that!" answered Benoni, still standing. "No, it was the Attorney. He's not in his office."

"No, he's not. . . . Oh, by the way, I don't know, it's his office hours. He must have just gone out."

"Ah, yes, yes, then perhaps he's at Sirilund or . . .?"

"He must have gone to see Mack, yes."

Meanwhile in her uneasiness Rosa had been putting things straight here and there; she had contrived to set

213

out her husband's opera-glasses on the table and casually left a parasol lying there too. It was the parasol of her young days. There lay the opera-glasses and the parasol, to make the room look a little less bare and more like a home with various things about it.

"I was all by myself," she explained, "so I thought I'd make myself useful and scrub the floor. Nikolai's mother is on a visit to her daughter."

Benoni knew that the old widow had gone to live with the daughter.

"And little Martha was getting so home-sick. . . . Oh, won't you sit down?"

"No, thanks, I can't spare the time, because of some foreigners coming to see me. No, it was only for the Attorney."

"Perhaps you'll meet him on the road," she said.

"Well, well, peace be with you!" said Benoni, and went out.

He did not meet Arentsen on the road and gave up the idea of looking for him at Sirilund. No, no, no! said Benoni to himself, and shook his head; how changed she was, how she seemed to be quite a different person! He retained the impression of his first sight of her, as she stood before him in the red petticoat which only reached to her calves.

When Benoni came home, the Sheriff's officer was already waiting for him; a little while after came the Attorney from town and the two Englishmen with their attendants. Benoni asked them all into his parlour; Sir Hugh appeared to be perfectly sober. When Benoni offered a dram all round, Sir Hugh curtly refused, which so offended Benoni that he said:

"Oh, no, I reckon this place isn't good enough for you."

The negotiations commenced. The Attorney sat and

smoothed out some papers with the palm of his hand as he spoke:

"Now about these rocks. Sir Hugh Trevelyan wishes to buy them, he has made an offer."

Benoni was still hurt; he said at once:

"I don't care about any offer. I don't care about selling the rocks, for that matter."

"What?" asked the Attorney in surprise.

"If you were to go over to Mack and make an offer for Sirilund, Mack would say to you: Sirilund is not for sale, then why do you come and bid for it?"

The Attorney said:

"It's not unlikely that Mack would sell if he got a high offer. And you have had a high offer for the rocks, Hartvigsen?"

"No," replied Benoni, dead against his conviction. "It's no offer at all."

"Five thousand dollars!"

"Well, but the rocks can stay there. I'm not pressed to sell them, you needn't think that."

Marelius of Torpelvik observed, as though he had anything to do with the business:

"You got the rocks yourself for a hundred dollars."

"Yes," replied Benoni; "but why didn't you buy them for fifty? You'd have got them for that. I paid more than was asked."

Sir Hugh was getting impatient and told the Attorney to ask what Benoni would sell the rocks for. Perhaps ten thousand?

Benoni took this to be a piece of sarcasm, and all he said was:

"I don't know. Anyway the rocks can stay there, they won't run away from me. And, over and above, there's silver in them."

Benoni

Pale with exasperation at all this chatter, Sir Hugh gasped:

"Oh."

This was not calculated to improve Benoni's temper.

"But is it your intention, Hartvigsen, that we should go on bidding everlastingly for the rocks?" asked the Attorney.

"I haven't asked for any bids," answered Benoni, irritated at the Englishman's superciliousness. "So that man has no call to sit here and snort any longer. He comes into a man's house and thinks the house belongs to him, and the man too."

The Attorney remarked in an undertone:

"But you must remember he's a foreigner, a gentleman of rank."

"What then!" retorted Benoni aloud. "Let him learn the ways of the country. When I was in Bergen and hailed people with 'Peace!' they didn't understand me. So I had to learn to say 'Good-day.'"

Sir Hugh looked infinitely bored with this man and his grievances. He guessed that it all came of a glass of brandy that he wouldn't drink; but it would never have occurred to him to drink that glass for the sake of a few thousand dollars. He got up, buttoned his check jacket and took up his hat with the salmon flies in it. As he was going he told his lawyer to ask if Benoni would sell for twenty thousand dollars.

Everybody in the room gave a start; only the two Englishmen did not turn a hair.

At that moment there was a knock at the door and Lightkeeper Schöning walked in. He made no ceremony, but went up to Benoni and said:

"If you don't believe me, look at this!"

With that he gave Benoni a paper. It was the report on the rocks.

Benoni

What must it have cost Lightkeeper Schöning to bring himself to hunt up that old document and make it public property! What a come-down for his own authority when he had to support it with another man's! And why hadn't he bought these rocks himself when they were to be had for nothing at all? Now it appeared that they really were worth something, since thousands were bid for them. Did Paul Schöning regret it now, and had he simply tried to conceal his own lack of enterprise in playing the wise man and exaggerating his contempt for money?

The mining expert had got hold of the report and was studying it eagerly. He pointed with his finger to one or two figures and showed them to Sir Hugh: the proportion of silver was higher than what he had found himself with his blowpipe. But of course it was possible that the samples had been picked for assay, you couldn't tell.

The Lightkeeper cut into this English conversation and stated in so many words that he and nobody else had sent the samples and that he had taken care to find average pieces of rock to send.

The Britons behaved as if they neither heard nor saw him. But their superciliousness was completely wasted on the Lightkeeper; oh, in cold and dogged contempt nobody could teach him anything!

"We haven't asked this man to interfere," Sir Hugh got his lawyer to say.

"And therefore," replied the Lightkeeper, turning to Benoni, "therefore you must not sell the rocks under a million."

This fabulous sum instantly swept all seriousness out of the room; even the Britons smiled scornfully. They still tried to pretend that this queer old fellow didn't exist; but, as he continued to interrupt, Sir Hugh through his lawyer requested that the man should go.

Benoni

So then the Lightkeeper found a chair and made himself at home.

"It is many, many years since I first had my eye on these rocks," he said. "But I had no use for them."

Sir Hugh, who stood putting on his gloves, could contain himself no longer and cried suddenly:

"It is *I* who discovered the rocks!"

And with that he looked savagely about him.

"Yes, of course, of course," said the Attorney.

Without having heard a syllable of the Englishman's outburst, the Lightkeeper continued:

"And Aron of the Hope had no idea of these things. I said to him half a generation ago: You have a silver field on your property. And when we got the report, there was no longer a doubt of it. Can't you buy the rocks? said Aron. No, I haven't the money for that, I answered; and besides, I have no use for all these riches, what should I do with them? You have children, said he. Yes, I replied, but my two girls are well married, both of them. Then you have a son, said he. Yes, but he'll die, I replied, he'll only live a few years. Since then the rocks have lain untouched."

Oh, how important it seemed to this miserable Lightkeeper to publish his sevenfold contempt for riches just at this juncture; it must have been that which made him so cynical! But perhaps at that moment there was nobody who suffered greater pangs in his heart.

The Attorney spoke in his professional manner:

"To put it plainly, Hartvigsen, you ought to answer the question whether contingently you would sell this mile of bare rock for twenty thousand dollars. I do not know whether it was an offer, probably not; in fact it could not be. I understood it as a suggestion thrown out in order to get a definite figure from your side."

Benoni

"Twenty thousand?" said the Lightkeeper. "One can hear how much you gentlemen understand of the matter. It's simply ridiculous. And a mile of rock, you say. Of course it isn't a mile of galena and silver, nor half that even; you gentlemen are mad! This isn't a question of hundreds of milliards' worth of silver. But it is a question of an extensive, over two per cent silver field which is not to be sold under a million."

"It might be," Benoni began slowly, addressing himself to the lawyer, "it might be that I'd sell if so be we . . . well, if we agreed on it."

What a fellow Benoni was to sit quietly in his chair and master the cold shivers that ran down his back! He didn't listen to the Lightkeeper's drivel about the million; but all these other big sums, five thousand, ten thousand, twenty thousand, stampeded all his fixed notions about money. He followed the progression one step further and his imagination stood still at forty thousand. But forty thousand was sheer insanity, and when the lawyer asked what sum they might possibly agree upon, Benoni came out with this forty thousand, mainly because it was on the tip of his tongue:

"For a matter of forty thousand dollars, it's not out of the question," said he.

And again everybody in the room gave a start; only the two Englishmen exchanged a hurried question and answer: How much? Eight, nearly nine thousand pounds.

The Lightkeeper rose from his chair:

"*Are* you out of your senses?" he hissed piercingly.

"Hush!" said some of the others; this was serious business and no moonshine. "Be quiet, sit down!" they said to him.

The Lightkeeper glared at Benoni with bulging eyes and gave one or two dry gulps:

"Forty thousand! You can get that from anybody, you

Benoni

can get it from your merchant in Bergen. God preserve me from a man like you!"

"Write!" came Sir Hugh's voice all at once. He was worn out with all this chatter and ready to burst with exasperation.

When the Attorney proceeded to draw up the document, the Sheriff's officer moved over to him and followed every word as it was written, absorbed in his calling, full of the law and its precepts.

"It's idiotic!" muttered Lightkeeper Schöning when all was lost. "It's brutish!" . . . He put on his hat and blundered out of the door without saying good-bye.

Nothing was heard but now and then a question and the answer to it: the title-deeds were to be made out in the name of the child Hugh Trevelyan of Torpelvik; the money was to be paid in a lump sum. "Where?" asked Benoni. Here. And within five weeks from date; it was already in the country, the mining expert was to fetch it from Christiania.

And the title-deeds were drawn up and signed.

XXVI

BENONI HARTVIGSEN is now at the head of Sirilund itself and Mack's partner. The way of it was this: Benoni had grown so rich, and where was the glory in moving to other parts and starting business and fish-curing and becoming a Mack among strangers? Here was his home and here he could get fun out of being a great man. It happened at this very time that Mack of Sirilund suddenly needed the help of just such a man as Benoni. His case was like that of his brother, Mack of Rosengaard; he had stomach trouble and had to start wearing a broad red band round his stomach when winter came. It was the result of a too princely style of living.

You see, Benoni could no more do without Mack than Mack without Benoni. Now there was this tremendous counting of the money for the silver field. When a few weeks had gone by and Sir Hugh came with the amount and a number of witnesses, Benoni in his hour of need had to apply to Mack of Sirilund and get him to be present on the great occasion. Were they genuine notes or forgeries? "Oh," said Mack, diving like a fish into this sea of money, "they're the right sort of notes," said he. Mack then offered to take the forty thousand dollars with him to Sirilund and keep them in his cash-box for the time being; but Benoni declined. "You shall have a receipt for them, of course," said Mack. "No, it's no good, I've got a roof of my own to put over them," replied Benoni. Then Mack said in conclusion: "My dear Hartvigsen, I only wanted to lend you a hand."

Benoni

But it was a dog's life keeping guard over such wealth against the dangers of fire and thieves. So when Arn Drier sailed the schooner *Funtus* to Bergen with the dried fish, Benoni also had business to take him there. His voyage was decided upon in Mack's office, and again Mack himself it was who proposed the happy plan.

"You ought to take a trip to Bergen," said Mack. "You could kill two birds with one stone."

"What may they be?"

"First, you could take your money there. It is needless and foolish to have a big capital like that lying in a stocking. You might send the money by mail; but it's just as well to take it yourself. If you do that, you can carry out your other piece of business at the same time: when the *Funtus* arrives with the fish, you can present yourself and receive five thousand dollars from my correspondent."

What had come over Mack? Benoni at the bottom of his heart had been prepared all the time to be put off with fresh evasions.

"But it isn't five thousand any longer," Benoni began, wishing to let him down easily.

Mack interrupted him:

"Of course it's five thousand dollars. Our little outstanding account is a separate affair. That was how you wished it."

Oh, that man, that master of the game, he never showed a moment's weakness! A faint suspicion crossed Benoni's mind that there must be some catch in this behaviour of Mack's; but the kind thoughtfulness and goodwill with which he was assailed induced him to mention another matter that he had at heart.

"Well, now I was thinking there might be a third reason for going to Bergen," said he.

"Oh?"

Benoni

"You see, I might be wanting a housekeeper or something of the sort."

"Don't be in a hurry to take a Bergen woman for that," Mack replied instantly. And God knows how he found this answer so quickly.

Benoni explained more precisely that it was so awkward the way things were at present, it would be uncomfortable after a while.

Mack went to the window and thought a moment, then turned round and said:

"I'll tell you something, my dear Hartvigsen; you ought to consult Rosa about that matter." . . .

When Benoni was in Bergen, Mack said to Rosa one day:

"Don't you know anybody who could come and keep house for Benoni?"

"No," she answered.

"Think it over. The man can't go on in this way."

"I'm sure he can get as many as he wants," she said.

They both thought awhile.

"You might do it," said Mack.

"I? You're crazy!"

"All right," he said. "Then we won't say any more about it." . . .

Benoni came back from Bergen. He had done his business and paid the money into the bank. And it was something of a bank, with gratings and iron doors and safes built into the vaults. Benoni had also kept his eyes open for a lady he might take home to the North to start a style of living in his house more in accordance with his rank; but nothing came of it. He met no other females than the daughters of the pavement and those who haunted the quays at night, and it might be no easy matter to make

Benoni

a happy choice among them. Besides which, Mack had warned him to have a care. "You had better consult Rosa about that matter," he had said. Perhaps Mack had some good intention in giving this advice.

Benoni went to Mack and asked whether Rosa knew what was to be done. "Oh, yes, that will all come right," said Mack. But all at once he began to talk about a stomach trouble that he was feeling for the first time, and with that he proposed to Benoni to take over a half-share in the whole business of Sirilund. Benoni could not believe his ears; he said: "What?" and "You're fooling?" Mack produced a complete scheme of partnership and ended by saying: "Think it over; perhaps it will not be so very long before you are sole master here."

A current of joy ran through Benoni at this proposal. He went home and thought over it a long time: ah, it was no longer a question of trifles, it was the biggest thing Benoni knew of in the whole world; he might become Master of Sirilund. What did it signify to be Admiral of the *Funtus,* to make a shot of herrings in the autumn and to sail to Lofoten and buy shiploads of fish in the winter, what was all that? Now he could hire men for that sort of work and he himself would only have to utter a word, point with his finger.

Benoni accepted.

A regular settlement was made between the brothers Mack before Benoni came into the business. In the course of this settlement it appeared that Mack of Sirilund was by no means an impoverished man. Far from it. And if he had been able to keep Benoni's five thousand dollars in peace, he would have been still more comfortably off. But Benoni's money had had to be paid now; otherwise what impression would he have had when Mack made him his great offer? In return Benoni appreciated this business exactitude and paid cash for the heirlooms

Benoni

and his store debts, so Mack had plenty of money in his cash-box.

Benoni continued to live at home in his own house. A calm had descended upon him after the excitement of the last few months, he began to get the hang of his great destiny. If only he had the housekeeper! It would not do to go on any longer with an old woman who came and went, the charwoman of his humble days. And what was Rosa's advice? That it would all come right—what would come right? Benoni himself never found a chance of speaking to her, she had once more vanished from his sight. Since that day in the spring, when he had walked into her room and had not yet become the mighty man he was, he had never met her. Now he would speak to her even if he had to go to church to do it. He had such a perfectly good reason.

And there you may see Benoni Hartvigsen on his way to church. Since his trip to Bergen he had taken to wearing different clothes and he was no longer the same person. Even before he became such a rich man, Benoni had gone the whole length in smart Sunday toggery; there was nothing more to be done in that direction. His top-boots had no rival in the country round, and more than two jackets no man could stand.

Then he noticed in Bergen that foot-gear tended in the direction of Mack's shoes and that it depended to a certain extent on the temperature whether one wore one or two jackets. When he had pondered this awhile, he brought back a considerable outfit suitable both for summer and winter.

"That's the way with all the big swells!" said the neighbours when they saw Benoni come to church. "He'd never let you see that he's what he is," they said. *"He* can afford two jackets, but does he wear them?"

So they bowed when he came near enough, and watched

Benoni

a chance to shake hands with him and pay him their compliments. And when Benoni stopped for a moment, he again had every right to stand erect as a monument and throw out his chest like a conqueror.

"If so be I come to you at the store one day and ask for a sack of flour to go on with . . ." says one, and stops short in his humility, without the pluck to finish his shamefaced request.

"A sack of flour?" replies Benoni; "we'll be able to manage that," he replies.

A woman who has known him from a child stands and looks at him as if he was the sun, and when he goes up to her with a nod and asks how they all are at home, she can scarcely answer for emotion. "Thank you for asking. Thank you for asking," is all she says, unable to give a separate account of each of her children, as it was her duty to do.

Benoni goes from group to group and has no need to give himself airs; everybody knows now what a great man he is and that it is out of pure kindness of heart he stops to speak to them. Puffed up with homage, open-handed with his help and happy in people's recognition of it, Benoni strides across the churchyard. Nor is he afraid of talking about the rocks that made him so rich; he says: "It isn't in everybody's line to buy big stretches of galena with silver in it. It takes a bit of foresight!—And by the same token it wants some knack to sell them again!" he goes on, showing his walrus teeth good-naturedly.

But the only one from whom in his heart he would have cared to have a little nod in these days of prosperity, she kept away.

And indeed it was more than striking that she never even showed herself at the store at Sirilund. For there too Benoni was now the master and he had by no means

Benoni

reduced the standing of the place by taking over half of it. Look at the goods there were before, and how many now came in by every mail-boat! Besides, in the drapery department all the shelves were now provided with glass fronts on account of the dust, and there were glass cases of haberdashery here and there on the counters. There seemed to be more money about everywhere. And as the business was now to serve two chiefs, it would have to be at least doubled; several big vessels were coming for the fish trade; a steamer had been chartered to bring grain for the mill direct from Archangel. In future more parishes would get their supplies of flour from Sirilund.

While Mack himself took charge of the office as before and hatched all the schemes as he well knew how to do, Benoni superintended the quays, the cooperage, the vessels and the mill. But, for all that, he did not deprive the store of his presence. He liked to come stalking in through the door and make all the customers bow. He found it a pleasing thing that all the people round the spirit counter dropped their voices from sheer respect and whispered when he appeared: "Hush, there's Hartvigsen himself!" That made him sociable and full of goodwill to all and he began to chaff them: "You there with the whole half-pint, can't you spare me a dram?" Ho-ho, what a joker that Hartvigsen was! If Steen the store clerk had refused some poor devil further credit, Benoni would quietly interpose in his omnipotence and say to Steen: "It's not so easy for folks; you must try and manage it!" And Steen the store clerk was no longer impertinent with Benoni; he answered respectfully: "Well, well, as you wish!" Then all the people in the store nodded to one another: it was a God's mercy that that Hartvigsen had arisen amongst them.

Benoni

But the one whose nod would have meant most to Benoni, she kept away.

Sometimes he would ask the blacksmith: "Is it for yourself or somebody else you're shopping to-day?" But if it was the wife of Villads the wharfinger who was doing Rosa's messages, Benoni stepped behind the counter and served her himself and contrived to give her extravagantly good measure.

XXVII

CHRISTMAS was coming on.

Attorney Arentsen had no more cases and expected none. He would have taken down his brass plate from the office door and gone off in the mailboat, but Rosa stopped him and said:

"Have you finished altogether with Aron of the Hope?"

"Yes."

"But supposing Levion of Torpelvik comes and wants to consult you while you're away?"

"He won't come."

No, Levion of Torpelvik did not come any more either, and he was the last. When Sir Hugh came and paid him for the two years' salmon-fishing, Levion had finally accepted the money. And so it looked as if that was the end of the long lawsuit. All the same, he had gone the next day to Attorney Arentsen for the last time and asked: "Is it so that we've still got the Supreme Court?" But Arentsen really could not be bothered to write any more about this case and give himself a lot of trouble; he answered Levion: "Everything has been done that can be done; now there's nothing left."

That miserable Nikolai Arentsen, he was going more and more to the bad. So long as the weather was warm enough, he made no particular difference between night and day; when he had been out and came home, he lay down on the bed irrespective of the hour. His laziness became terrible, it passed into obstinacy, into energy: for a week he never took off his clothes or his shoes, but slept wherever he happened to lie down. He was not

Benoni

ashamed in his wife's presence; why should he give himself airs before her? Rosa and he had been married a year and a half; for over five hundred days they had not been able to avoid seeing one another's faces and hands and hearing one another's familiar words. They knew each other so thoroughly, there was not the slightest hope that one day they might give one another a small surprise by some variation of the day before.

"I might perhaps have got a job at Post Benoni's store," said Young Arentsen in his hopelessness. "They'll be wanting extra hands for the Christmas trade."

But Rosa opposed this too. She had good grounds for anxiety if her husband got behind the various counters at Sirilund.

"You can't mean that," she said. "A lawyer can't very well turn store clerk."

"But what the hell do you want me to do?" he cried irritably. "Last year you wouldn't let me apply for the post of fishery magistrate either."

Last year it was another matter, they were newly married then, and Nikolai had just made his promising start as an attorney. Oh, there was all the difference in the world! She replied:

"Can't you take a post as fishery magistrate this year?"

"Take! Do you think one has only to *take* a post like that?"

"Well, apply for it then."

"I have applied," said Young Arentsen. "I didn't get the post, my application was refused. My conduct as attorney had not been such as to recommend me for magistrate. Now you know."

Pause.

Young Arentsen went on:

"Life comes to some people—oh, what's the use of

Benoni

talking about it? It comes like a soft white angel to some people. To me too the angel came. And began at once to caress me with a curry-comb."

Pause.

"I have never denied," he began again, "I have never denied that Post Benoni could build a dovecote or even two. He could afford it before and he can still better afford it now. On the other hand, I denied that Post Benoni was a husband for you. But possibly I was wrong there."

"I can't understand why I should have to suffer for it like this," said Rosa mournfully.

"No," he replied, "why should you understand it? And why should I mention it, as it isn't really you who have to suffer? But why should I suffer for it either? And why anything at all?"

They had been into these questions many times before, there was nothing new in them, they were familiar past bearing to both of them.

He ended by speaking rather more plainly, by studiously choosing words of another kind:

"So I have spoilt your life, little Rosa, that is how it is. Your whole life."

To this she made no reply, but went and sat by the window and looked out to sea.

Well, she might have made some answer; surely she was not going to believe what he said? Of course it was no more true that he had spoilt her life than she his, for that matter. And why did she go and sit over there? Did she think there were more words of this new kind coming? He rose and buttoned up his coat.

"Are you going out?"
"Yes. What should I do here?"

Pause.

Benoni

"That's just it," she then said; "you really ought to have more to do here and go out less."

This was, at all events, nothing new; oh, how he had heard it hundreds of times before! And he had answered it every time; but evidently she still stuck to it firmly. It was enough to kill a man.

"You know my opinion on that point," he said. "You're always thinking of those quarterns. And I who can put away two whole bottles without its upsetting me! I once went with two bottles of brandy and some goes of toddy under my waistcoat. Yes. So you imagine that if I had any work to do, I couldn't do it just as well in spite of these quarterns. They're not what makes the difference, it lies much deeper. And as far as that goes, I may as well tell you what's at the bottom of it all: the trouble is that we ought to have stayed engaged all our lives, we ought. That's the root of the trouble. We ought never to have got married."

"I dare say you're right," she said.

This acquiescence was something new on her part, never before had she thus fallen in with his train of thought. He seemed to catch sight of an opening before him. In Heaven's name, he could breathe now! His voice was lively and downright cheerful:

"Well, wasn't I right? Can you go at this moment to the piano and play something to amuse yourself? No; we have no piano. We haven't anything at all, we're living on our credit at Sirilund. And you know in your heart that it isn't the quarterns that are to blame for that. The fact is, we are paralysed, both of us. Paralysis has seized us. First it attacked my feet: I wouldn't be bothered to walk; then my hands, finally my mind. . . . When I come to think of it, it was just in the reverse order that I got paralysed, but that's no matter. And there you are, you've come into line with me now. You understand what I'm saying, you can enter into it, it isn't Egyptian to you—a couple of years ago you wouldn't have grasped a word of it. And perhaps I shouldn't either."

"No, I don't understand," Rosa protested, shaking her head. "Not all of it, oh, no. Are we paralysed? I'm more inclined to think it's you who were born so. No, not born so, but become so. So wouldn't you have done better if you'd left me alone when you came back?"

Aha, it was all over with he acquiescence!

"I might make you a caustic answer to that if I chose," he said. "I might say, I didn't leave you alone for the reason that I had the honour to be in love with you again."

"You were nothing of the sort. Oh, no. You were paralysed even then."

"And that is why I don't say it. On the other hand, I say bluntly that I meant to have you. Yes. But there is no doubt it was Post Benoni's fault."

She did not look up. This too straightforward talk was another of the things she had heard before. He ended with one of his daily phrases:

"When Post Benoni proposed, I proposed too. It makes a difference when there's somebody else, an enormous difference. If you see a thing lying on the ground, it is worth nothing to you. It's only when somebody else comes along and wants to pick it up that you think it valuable and go for it."

Pause. Nothing told on either of them now. Rosa was thinking for the moment that it was twelve o'clock, time to put on the potatoes for dinner.

"Oh, no, if it was the quarterns, I'd cut them out all right," he said.

"No, you wouldn't even take the trouble to do that."

Benoni

And why should he? It wasn't the fault of the drinks, so why should he bother to cut them out? Wasn't such logic enough to kill a man? Weary of wrangling, he forced himself to say:

"Oh, no, I wouldn't even take that trouble, I don't trouble about anything. I did a little at first, but that soon came to an end. It was all over when we got married; neither of us ought to have married. I ought to have taken the mail-boat South again at once." . . .

So they had had their bout of squabbling again and Young Arentsen walked out of the house.

Fine weather; a column of smoke rose far out, it was the mail-boat coming. Yes, of course, he ought to have gone South again at once and not taken root here; he ought never to have come here at all, but stayed where he was. He would have made some shift for a living as he had done before in the big city where he was up to all the ropes.

He went past Sirilund and came to the smithy. The blacksmith and the lawyer exchanged a few hurried remarks and turned their pockets out to show each other that they hadn't a penny to-day. Then Young Arentsen strolled back to Sirilund; he might shake off some of his humour by dropping into the bar. Not that he wouldn't cheerfully have done without; but, you see, it wasn't the quarterns that were to blame for anything. What was the sense in going straight home again and sitting down in his office to look at a lot of meaningless documents?

Mack beckoned to him from the window; Young Arentsen pretended not to see and was going past. Then Mack suddenly appeared at the office door.

"Come in," said Mack, opening the door. There was a hurried look about him.

"No, thanks," said Young Arentsen, and was going on.

Benoni

"Come in," repeated Mack.

Not a word more did he say, but Young Arentsen followed. They went into the office. Mack said straight away:

"My dear Nikolai, this won't do. It's too rough on you and Rosa both. Will you have some money to take you South again?"

Young Arentsen stammered: "Why, perhaps ... South? ... I don't understand ..."

Mack looked at him with his cold eyes and only added in a few words that the credit at the store couldn't go on for ever. On the other hand, the mail-boat was now coming into harbour. And here was the money. ...

Next day Rosa came to Mack and asked, cautiously, just feeling her way: "Nikolai went out so early this morning. He said ... he was talking about ..."

Nikolai? He left yesterday in the mail-boat. He had business in the South, a case. Didn't Rosa know about it?

"No. Well, that is ... In the mail-boat? Didn't he say anything?"

"A big case, he said."

A minute's silence; Rosa stood bewildered in the middle of the room.

"Yes, he has talked about going South," she said. "So this case must have come on very suddenly."

"I don't think you ought to go back to the blacksmith's now," said Mack.

And Rosa stayed. One day, several days. A week passed, and still she stayed. It was brighter here at Sirilund, plenty of people, traffic and life. There was Villads the wharfinger just coming up from the quays for something or other; seeing Rosa at the window, he took off his hat. Rosa had known him since she was a child; she went out and asked him:

Benoni

"You haven't any message for me, have you, Villads?"

"H'm. Only that the Attorney told me to tell you he got on board the steamer all right."

"Nothing more?"

"No."

"Yes, he had to go South; he had a big case on. So he got on board all right?"

"Got on board fine. I was in my boat and saw him."

So Rosa lived at Sirilund and was like a girl again and knew everybody. And Sven Watchman was there likewise. He did not sing though, or raise a merry noise as when he was a bachelor; that kind of thing would not do now. But he had his town manners, he bowed and spoke so politely; Rosa enjoyed a chat every time she met him. She paid a visit to their little room to see Ellen and the baby. Now there it was: Ellen Parlourmaid had had this baby, this little boy with the brown eyes, and nobody could make out why his eyes should be brown. "There's nothing about it at all," said Ellen, "except that I was lying here where Fredrik Mensa is. And he's so queer with his brown eyes," she said.

And Fredrik Mensa was queer enough, and no mistake. He never died; on the contrary, he lay there all the time full of activity, looking as if he had made up his mind to start a second life the very next morning. The child's screaming was a great puzzle to him. Every time he thought it was something he had caught sight of, and he tried to get hold of it with his hands. Finding nothing, he thought it must be out in the harbour; he tried to frighten it away and screamed at it; when it screamed back, he answered again and again. In his excitement he continued to clutch at the air; he had no power over his hands, they jostled each other clumsily and got mixed up; then they fell out, one hand felt it had caught the other and started to squeeze it. Now

Benoni

he had horrible yellow nails like the bowls of horn teaspoons, and when he dug these nails in, it hurt him and he said "Uff" and swore. Then at last one hand got the better of the other and threw it down. Then Fredrik Mensa laughed with delight. But while the fight was going on, he discovered lots of happy words to describe his feelings: "Smoke on the ceiling? Haha. Don't row any more, Mons. Aye aye, aye aye, aye aye."

So there lay Fredrik Mensa in his vocation, yelling his bestial imbecility into the ears of a new-born babe from the first day of its life. And the maids who went on filling him with food never forgot to treat him with respect and called him by his name.

"Now Mensa must be good and take this," they say.

Then an excessively thoughtful look comes over him; it is as though he had to declare his religious convictions.

"Da da da da da," says Fredrik Mensa.

XXVIII

BUT though it was winter now and the weather was cold, Mack of Sirilund had not started the broad red band round his stomach. Not at all. It was like a miracle, his insidious stomach trouble must have stopped half-way and turned back. Mack had never shown more talent for keeping alive than now, nor had he ever dyed his hair and beard with greater care. He thought of everything. When the new big vessels were bought, all their cabins were enlarged and painted in bright colours. "It has a good effect on the skipper," said Mack; "and not only that but it reflects credit on the owners." Besides this, Mack had taken a great fancy to a small steamer he had seen for sale in the papers; as soon as the Lofoten fish business showed signs of extension, he would vote for buying a steamer.

Nor did he forget to direct the affairs of his household with a fatherly hand, as had always been his way. When Benoni proposed his old mate Sven Watchman as skipper of one of the new vessels, it struck Mack at once that in that case Sven and Ellen could not go on living in the little room. A big new home was got ready for them at the other end of the servants' hall, where the clerk of the court had had his office during the Sessions.

This year Mack did not sell all the feathers and down from his bird rocks. He had some of the finest quality set apart to make a wonderful feather-bed for himself, and it was to be his new bed for the bath-tub. Young Petrine of Torpelvik, the latest parlour-maid, who was

Benoni

only in her seventeenth year, she couldn't be expected to haul about heavy old things, and, besides, it was an idea of Mack's to have a feather-bed for his bath with every new parlour-maid; so that there might be a green one for a change, when it had been red or blue or yellow before. Oh, but a terrible thing happened to the feathers of this new bed. They had been laid out to dry and curl nicely on some boards in the wash-house, and one morning they were all burnt. Nobody had done it, nobody could make out how it happened. And Ellen, who had once been Ellen Parlour-maid, she made the worst outcry over the disaster and said that she hadn't done it. "But I don't know what he wants with another feather-bed either," she said; "and he's not going to have another feather-bed at all!" she said to Bramaputra. But Mack, he thought otherwise. Christmas was coming, aye, Christmas Eve was coming, and he knew what he wanted. He had a notice put up in the store that he was giving a good price for fine feathers and down for immediate delivery. And was not that the same as issuing an order to come along with your feathers? Sure enough, any quantity of feathers came along to Sirilund those days, till Mack himself said Stop.

And Rosa, she stayed on. And Mack would not have been the fatherly person he was if he had not had a care for Rosa's welfare among the rest. Why couldn't she agree to keep house for Benoni? She was free now. He tried to make it easier for her, to make it look more attractive in her eyes; he said:

"There's another reason why you ought to think about going to keep house for my partner . . ." And he said partner in order to raise Benoni as high as possible.

"What reason is that?"

"A reason so great that it ought to be enough in itself. You were so fond of the child, of Martha, weren't

Benoni

you? Well, my partner will adopt Martha if he can get someone to look after things for him."

"Has he said so?"

"Yes."

"I can't go," replied Rosa, shaking her head.

Mack went on:

"It's splendid of Hartvigsen, I think. Martha's father, our worthy Steen in the store, has in fact not always been very nice to him; but . . ."

"I can't go," repeated Rosa. "It's impossible."

"But at any rate you might help us a little in the store at Christmas time: then he would have a chance of talking to you himself."

"No, I can't help in the store this year," said Rosa, as before; "I must go home."

So Rosa went home to the parsonage.

And Christmas came.

But when Mack was to have his usual bath fixed up on Christmas Eve, it appeared that the wonderful new feather-bed was all in order, but a sad hole had been punched in the mighty zinc tub. And the blacksmith had got drunk and could not solder it. And nothing would go right that day; the tradition was broken. But how was it that the blacksmith came to be so dead-drunk just when Mack himself wanted him? He had been staggering about ever since the afternoon, and then he had been invited in by Ellen, who had once been parlour-maid; and Sven Watchman was not there, but Ellen had treated the blacksmith so liberally to spirits that the old man had rolled on to the floor. Ah, that Ellen Parlour-maid, such was her despair at what she had done that she asked in her grief whether they couldn't plug the bath-tub with a little thick porridge. "Oh, no," said Bramaputra. "But can't we take a needle and thread and sew it up?" asked Ellen, and then she began to laugh

Benoni

hysterically in her despair at what she had done to the blacksmith. But Mack, he was ready at once with another plan: he was going to take one of the *Funtus'* boats up to his room and fill it with bath water and spread the feather-bed over its bottom to make a fine couch. Sven Watchman was sent for; but when he appeared before the housekeeper and received his orders, he said: "Why, bless you!"—holding his cap right down to his knees—"none of these boats has been put in the water since the autumn, they're as leaky as a lot of outrageous swine!" said Sven Watchman politely, and made his bow.

So nothing would go right at all that day.

And didn't it seem as if everything was bound to go wrong this year? When Mack opened the letter from his daughter Edvarda in Finland, the yearly letter she wrote home for Christmas, he gave a great start and went straight to the window to think. It was a short letter: Edvarda was now a widow. She was coming home in the spring.

Mack controlled himself, received his guests, received Lightkeeper Schöning as usual, received Benoni, who was now his partner and head of the firm like himself and so fantastically rich with it all. Mack led him to the sofa and thanked him over and over again for coming that evening. He turned to the lightkeeper and asked:

"But Madam Schöning?"

"I don't know," replied the Lightkeeper without looking round for her.

"She's coming, isn't she?"

"Who?" said the Lightkeeper.

It was all of no consequence to him, he despised these questions and this Ferdinand Mack and all his house. And there sat the former mine-owner Benoni Hartvigsen blinking his blue eyes and exuding his stupid opulence from the sofa. In the dining-room the maids could be

Benoni

heard laying the table, full of inward ecstasy at its being this particular evening of the year! Oh, if there were not a few pictures on the walls, this place would be insufferable!

Then came Madam Schöning. She made an excuse for coming too early. "You're not at all too early, my dear Madam Schöning," said Mack; "your husband has been here a quarter of an hour." "Has he?" she replied, and didn't see her husband anywhere, didn't see the shadow of her husband.

At table Mack made his ceremonious speeches. Of his daughter he said that he hoped Baroness Edvarda remembered her old home and would visit it in the spring. . . . Not a word of the catastrophe; it was Christmas Eve.

Then Mack proposed Benoni's health, the very good health of his partner, who had been so kind as to come this evening. After that the health of the Lightkeeper and his wife, and finally that of all his household. And all this army of people who made their living at Sirilund sat like children listening to Mack's moving words; Bramaputra even used her handkerchief. But Fredrik Mensa could not be brought to table in his bed; oh, but he was not left to lie by himself on such an evening, not at all; a woman sat there feeding him and reading prayers to him and agreeing with him through thick and thin. On the other side of the room lay Ellen's little boy, who had to look after himself; he yelled on and off, smiled, kicked and yelled again. But he disturbed the other two at their prayers quite a lot and Fredrik Mensa called out once or twice in a fury: "King David, King David! damn him; ho!" to which the woman answered: "Yes you're quite right there, remember King David in the Bible!". . . For the sake of appearances Ellen looked in for a moment from the dining-room,

Benoni

turned the child over and went out again. She had other things to think of, things that would happen by and by: when the guests were gone, the searching was bound to begin. But never in this world should that chit of a girl, that Petrine of Torpelvik, have a chance of slipping a silver fork under the lining of her petticoat. . . .

Benoni asked Mack:

"Well, so Rosa didn't know of any housekeeper for me, did she?"

How awkward it was for him, and what a come-down for this mighty man to show it! He wanted a gentlewoman to keep house for him and couldn't find her for all his money.

Mack asked him to wait till the spring:

"Dear friend, wait till the spring, I beg you. In the spring my daughter is coming home, and the two ladies are very good friends." . . .

During the holidays Benoni meant to make a trip across the common to the neighbouring parish church. He did it to pass the time; he might just as well hear what the great preacher Barfod had to say at one of these many Christmas services. As it no longer suited his position to go on foot, he got a horse and sledge from Mack, and with them he got the loan of Mack's coat with the sealion skin lining. "I haven't got myself a fur coat yet," said Benoni to Sven Watchman, who sat behind in the dicky. Benoni had been doubtful about getting Sven to drive him, for now the said Sven was a married man and, moreover, had been promoted to skipper of a big vessel. "You won't care to drive me, will you?" asked Benoni. "It would be a nice shame if I didn't drive Hartvigsen," was Sven's answer.

This was in the yard at Sirilund.

They went round by Benoni's house, where they put a case of bottles and a hamper in the sledge. Benoni came out with his sea-boots and told Sven Watchman to put them on. And they were the famous sea-boots with the glazed tops in which Benoni himself had swaggered about so many a time.

"Put them on," said Benoni.

He had got into the habit of speaking in a mild and decided tone, his riches had braced him up, given him more backbone, made his clothes more dignified, transformed a good deal of his language. Ah, what money could do to make a person of Benoni! But when Benoni asked Sven Watchman to put on the sea-boots, the latter replied in his old way:

"Then what will you have for yourself?"

Benoni stuck his feet into fur-lined boots from Bergen with dogskin tops. Then Sven put on the sea-boots and they were like ornaments on his legs.

"If they fit, you can keep them," said Benoni.

And Sven Watchman answered:

"That's much too much again. They'll be Sunday boots for the rest of my life."

Then they drank a few drams and drove off.

On the road they chatted about one thing and another; they went over ground where Benoni knew every juniper and every fir and every rock. There he had walked in sunshine and in rain, carrying the Royal Mail in a bag with a lion on it, and there, worse luck, was Holla, where he and Rosa parson's daughter had taken shelter. Oh, that Holla!

"Can't you sing a bit?" he asked over his shoulder.

"Sing? H'm. I don't seem to have any gift that way now," replied Sven. "There's such a lot of things."

And when they opened the case a little farther on and took another dram or two, Sven Watchman was so strangely soft-hearted and so rueful in his speech, it

Benoni

was just as if he was fasting and couldn't stand strong drink.

"It so happens, to tell the truth, that I've had nothing to eat to-day," he said. "It's a shameful thing to say."

The hamper came out, with Christmas dainties, bannocks.

"Why haven't you had anything to eat?"

"It was my own fault. But there's such a lot of things!" replied Sven. He gave Benoni to understand that there had been a little tiff between him and Ellen that morning, so that he couldn't get any food down.

They drove on and on. Sven Watchman said:

"If I had my diamond back and could diddle you out of a case of glass from the store, I've been thinking of taking to the road again."

Benoni turned and faced him:

"Now that you're to be skipper!"

Sven wagged his head.

"And with a family and a child and all!"

"Yes," he answered, "that's all right, but . . ."

The good Sven Watchman had been married for six months or more, he had given up singing of Sorosi Lasses and he no longer danced along the road. That never occurred to him now. Six months seemed an endless time. He had got the one he wanted, true; but all his happy suspense and impatience was gone, he was glad now for every day he got rid of. And every morning he awoke to the same state of having nothing to look forward to, two hundred times in succession this had repeated itself: he had got up and Ellen had got up, their clothes were the same, they put them on as they had done yesterday. Ellen looked out of the window to see if Mack's two window-blinds were down and all in order. Then she said the same insufferably familiar

Benoni

words about the weather, but that was only to hide the direction of her eyes. They grudgingly made room for each other in the cramped space, each waiting for the other to be ready first and out of the way; and they separated without a word. Two hundred times. And there would be thousands of times to come.

"You're not like your old self," said Benoni. "In the spring, when you bring your vessel home from Lofoten, you'll have a big new home to go into."

"It's too much, far too much."

"Is the child getting on?" asked Benoni.

"Yes, he's getting on. He has brown eyes, but he's a pretty child, I like him all right."

"Have you ever held him?"

"No."

"Haven't you held him?"

"I've thought of doing, but . . ."

"You should take and hold him a bit," Benoni advised.

"Oh, you mean that?"

"Yes, I mean that. As for the brown eyes, they—well, that's not to be helped, but . . ."

Then they were there, driving into the yard of the parsonage in a cloud of new-fallen snow.

A gentleman in furs, Hartvigsen himself; two of the men came and took out the horse. Walk in, please, walk in! No, thanks. Benoni was fretting inwardly at an old memory that gave him no peace; once upon a time he had been forced to sign a certain hard-hearted declaration at this parsonage, and then the same declaration had been read out by the Sheriff at his own church door. And since then Rosa had been his sweetheart, and afterwards had thrown him over and married another, married Nikolai the parish clerk's son. Aye, aye. . . .

Benoni in all his glory passes through the churchyard,

Benoni

gently parting the knots of people, who make way for him with a bow; everybody knows him. A message comes, won't Hartvigsen be good enough to look in at the parsonage and have something warm? No, thanks; he has business to see to; after service perhaps he'll be glad to come. He has no business; but so great a man can always find something among all these people; for instance, he has to find crews for Lofoten for the new vessels. There is no need for him to take the first step either; if he is not already surrounded by applicants, it is because of the deep respect they feel. Then they come, one after another, take off their caps and hesitate to put them on again, though it is pretty cold: Couldn't Hartvigsen do them the favor of keeping a place for them in one of the boats? And Benoni stands like a monument in fur coat and fur boots and is a kind, warm-hearted master to them all. "I'll think about it," he answers, and makes a note of the name; "come to me in a few days' time. Of course I mustn't forget my own neighbours; but we'll see."

There comes Pastor Barfod in full canonicals and stops by Benoni and asks him on no account to pass his door. Benoni thanks him, he'll try and find time after service, and is the Pastor quite well?

There, Benoni Hartvigsen couldn't have spoken to Pastor Barfod like that in days gone by.

Rosa was not to be seen. So perhaps she would not be in church to-day. Good.

But there she was after all. Benoni took off his fur cap and Rosa went past, red as fire. Poor Rosa, she hadn't been able to restrain her curiosity, she couldn't resist seeing Benoni in his furs. She went in by the vestry door.

Benoni stood there awhile to collect himself; then he said to the last of the applicants: "Well, well, I dare

Benoni

say you're not so well off; you must come down one of these days and you shall have some gear." "Bless you!" said the man. And Benoni went into church.

It was with deliberate intent that he took his seat immediately inside the door. The congregation opened their eyes: *he* could have sat right up by the chancel arch, but he did not! Rosa sat in the parsonage pew and looked in his direction; she turned red again and slowly paled. She had on her blue fox.

He unbuttoned his fur coat. He knew very well that the place he had taken was not meant for the gentry; not only the Sheriff, but some small traders from the outlying stations, sat higher up. But Benoni filled his seat well and lent dignity to his humble place for the time. He knew that more than one of those present must be feeling ashamed and wishing they sat far below Hartvigsen, the mighty Hartvigsen; would they had never gone to church that day!

As soon as the sermon was over, some of the common people walked out; Benoni buttoned his fur coat and went with them. He would not torture Rosa any longer; people had been looking at her and at him and at her again and calling to mind their old engagement. How she has thrown herself away! they must have been thinking. Benoni went down to his sledge, and Sven Watchman was on the heels of his master and asked if he was to put the horse in. Yes, right away! But the rumour spread that Hartvigsen was getting into his sledge; by all that's holy, he's just going to drive home! The parson's wife comes running down the steps, heedless of the cold and the fresh snow, and goes straight up to Benoni, gives him her hand frankly and begs him not to refuse her a visit. They had been so glad to see him come.

While they are standing there, Rosa comes out of

Benoni

church. Poor Rosa, she must have been curious to see whether Benoni would go straight home again. Now she is coming. Her mother calls to her:

"Hartvigsen absolutely insists on going. Come and help me to get him to stay."

Rosa is in such confusion, she is all to pieces and can only say:

"Won't you do us the pleasure of coming in?"

Benoni doesn't make himself more important than he is, there is no need for that; he makes no other excuse but that it is a long way and the days are short, he must start at once.

"There is a moon now," says Rosa.

"Yes, there's a moon now," says her mother too.

"I don't know?" says Benoni to Sven Watchman, and gives him a questioning look. "Do you think we can wait a bit?"

Sven Watchman knows how to behave in such company, he pulls off his cap, bows and replies:

"I'm sure we have time and light enough in that case."

"You see, I'm not altogether my own master these times," Benoni explains as he accompanies the ladies; "I have plenty to do with fitting out all these vessels."

How strange it was! Here was Rosa, here, walking close beside him, and, soon after, she sat down in the same room with him, and listened to what he said, and looked at him now and then, and even answered a word or two. When Pastor Barfod came in from church and they sat down to table, Benoni was helped by Rosa to one thing after another which she saw he wanted. It was all so wonderful, as in a dream. He fought against a disagreeable uncertainty: what tone ought he to speak in and how often ought he to look at her? Yet he had been engaged to this woman, had kissed her, built a house for her; they had only just missed being married.

Benoni

After dinner the parson and his wife retired for a nap. That was the usual thing. But that left Benoni alone in the room with his old sweetheart! "Won't you play a little, please?" he said; "but perhaps it will disturb the old people?" Yes, it will do that, she must have thought; probably it will disturb the old people. But she sat down to play all the same. He thought it was lovely, he had never heard the like, and he felt it was a tender act on her part to play to him like that. She swayed her shoulders now to the right, now to the left, her hair was so thick at the back, and below it was her neck, her white neck.

He thanked her so nicely. "That's the prettiest thing I've heard," he said. When she had finished, they both sat for a while not knowing what to say. "Ah, I reckon you had to sit at it many a good time before you learnt to play," he said. "Oh, yes," she said with a little smile, "but I'm not much good at it anyhow." They chatted about various things, his riches helped him out, he thought of what he was and gave expert answers about the new vessels when she asked. The time was passing, passing quickly. Benoni guessed that the old people would be back directly. Well, he had a question to ask her, he was within his rights and he said:

"I don't know whether Mack has spoken to you about something for me?"

He sat and looked at her and saw the little pucker appear above her nose.

"Mack thought you might possibly know of a housekeeper for me."

"No," she answered.

"No, no. It was only in case you knew of somebody in the South. There was no more meant than that."

She shook her head:

"No, I don't know of anybody."

Benoni

Pause. Benoni looked at his watch. Why didn't the old people come? He didn't care to explain the blunder as simply and solely Mack's idea. But, after all, there was no great harm done. He got up, approached a picture on the wall and looked at it. Then he went on to another picture. Rosa seemed so lonely over there. He asked politely:

"Well, I suppose I may give them your love at Sirilund?"

"Yes, please."

When the old people came in, the young people had just spoken these words. They were to be the last for a long time. After coffee Benoni took his leave and drove home. Now it was no use waiting till Edvarda came home in the spring; the matter was settled.

There was a bright moon and northern lights; Benoni was once more on familiar ground. At the top of Holla he could see there was a breeze catching the fresh snow and whirling it aloft.

"*Borre ækked,*" came a greeting from the road.

Benoni answered and drove on. . . .

Spring came and Mack's daughter Edvarda stepped ashore from the mail-boat. But that is another story and another little book, the name of which is ROSA.

THE END

A NOTE ON THE TYPE IN WHICH THIS BOOK IS SET

The type in which this book has been set (on the Linotype) is Old Style No. 1. In design, the face is of English origin, by MacKellar, Smith and Jordan, and bears the workmanlike quality and freedom from "frills" characteristic of English old styles in the period prior to the introduction of the "modern" letter. It gives an evenly textured page that may be read with a minimum of fatigue. Old Style No. 1 was one of the first faces designed and cut by the Linotype Company, and it is still one of the most popular.

SET UP, ELECTROTYPED AND PRINTED BY THE VAIL-BALLOU PRESS, INC., BINGHAMTON, N. Y. · PAPER MANUFACTURED BY W. C. HAMILTON & SONS, MIQUON, PA., AND FURNISHED BY W. F. ETHERINGTON & CO., NEW YORK · BOUND BY THE H. WOLFF ESTATE, NEW YORK ·